'THE RAGING HORMONES'

By

Ron S. King.

'THE RAGING HORMONES'

ISBN: 978-1-84753-211-4

PREFACE.

Some time back, due to my Grandsons' peculiar behaviour and his insistent questioning about certain young ladies, I realised he was undergoing the transition , called 'Puberty'… The magical discovery that a 'Winkle' is not simply for seeing how far one might urinate.

This set me to thinking about puberty and its effects on a young man's life; it also set me thinking about my own 'Voyage of Discovery', the transition from boy to man.

A strange fact was that I could not remember any effects at all. There were no facial disfigurations or dysfunctional exhibitions, to jar my memory.

Then… It dawned on me; through my time of puberty; I had been enormously attracted to my teachers, no matter how hideous or the age (female, of course!). I was also drawn to Nurses (Those starched uniforms and strong legs in black stockings sent shivers through me…And still do!).

Further to introspection, I then realised that we chaps never really evolve, we are 'Peter Pan's'; forever in the throes of an evolvement of puberty.

For this reason, I decided to create a boy who would go through this stage of life… Helped along by an elder sibling and others, who helped to soothe the passions of the 'Raging Hormones.'.

Ron. S. King.

DEDICATION.

I would like to dedicate this book to every man 'Jack' of us, who has had to undergo the horrific hormonal changes, which enforce us to see the world in a different light; when dreams and games, such as 'Pirates' and 'Cowboys and Indians', become 'Doctors and Nurses'!

I dedicate it to we brave chaps who, in our manhood, realise that we are not the 'Heroes' of our childish imaginations… But rather an inferior race of beings, subject to the whims of our sexual appetites and the ladies who understand our needs…

CHAPTER ONE.

‘IN THE BEGINNING’

In the beginning…(There is always a beginning and that is where I shall start!)… I shall endeavour to introduce you to the main cast of this play. As the 'Teller' and the 'Director' of this piece, I shall give myself no name or title, just a simple introductory effort…

Thus, in the beginning; there is ME…

I will admit to you, dear readers, that I am a most tiresome child. I live in a world of questions, a life of riddles which would all but destroy the mind of children, who, unlike me, live in a world of simple enjoyment.

Perhaps, had I been an only child, friendless and alone, I would have, no doubt, been under the supervision of an army of therapists, examined daily by the brainiest of psychologists… Indeed; my brains would have been scattered; except that…

…Except that I had a gift from God, a most highly divine elder sibling who could, if he so wished, answer any question I proposed.
I adored him, this elder brother who ruled my very world. There was no other of such worth in my eyes, of no higher value, or more worthy of being cast in

marble, to shame even the beautiful statue of David by Michelangelo.

As the first-born son of my parents, my brother had every right to adorn the heavens, to rise in such elevation, that I felt compelled to lower myself in estimation whenever his shadow darkened my path. Even the sharp clip to my ear was a small price to pay for his presence, the pain a simple reminder that even I, in such low esteem, was not ignored by such a high holiness.

My world consisted of, foremost, my godlike elder sibling, whom I describe often as… 'He, who walks the heavens'.

Then, next comes my very best of friends and 'Blood-Brother, Spotty Watson. Though not brave, in the sense that he would never be drawn into 'Fisticuffs' with the other youths in school; he would always, as a true friend, offer to be my 'Second', if ever I were to be challenged to a duel.

Needless to say, while I admired, as all young boys do, the raw bravado of the 'Fighting-Man', I did not have the build nor the heart to activate myself in the challenging world of 'Fisticuffs'. Suffice it to state that Spotty Watson and I were more sensitive in nature than others in our class at school.

Spotty is followed by his father, whom, next to my sainted brother, has the most ingenious of minds. Spotty refers to his father as the 'Teller of Tall Tales', which gives his father the serious rank of 'High Thinker'.
Spotty Watson's father dubs himself as the 'Poor man's Philosopher' and 'The Pleb-Psychologist', words which seem to be very grand, in my estimation. Spotty is so proud of him, as, no doubt, I would be, should I have had such a wise man for my father.

That, I suppose, brings me to my parents…

My Mother; a rather large lady, of a very Christian nature… And my Father, a small man, small of nature and small in the art of enthusiasm.

There… With that done, as an introduction to the cast… We may now, get on with the play…

And so… In continuation…

I was once informed by 'He, who walks the heavens', it was improper to ask another their age and so, with this in mind, I shall not inform you of my mine… Suffice it to state that I am, as Spotty Watson's father calls Spotty and I, a 'Mid-Term Cocoon Element'. He once explained that we were cught in a time-warp, wrapped in a cocoon of spun

silk, neither boys nor men, neither reasonable to our procreative urges, nor un-sensitive to sexual sensibilities, I was 'Mid-Term'.
While I never seem to get the 'Gist' of his speech, I am sure there is something going on within my frame.

Writing of ages…

Spotty Watson's father had once informed Spotty that young children always added the half-years to their age as an impatient rush into their future. It also seemed the virile assured all of their prime-time through actions of speech and dress.
Those, he had added, of middle-age, disliked to mention that fact, as it reminded them of their lost prime and the ill-nature that such remembrance gave. Those of an advanced age would be quick to tell all and sundry of their time in life, simply because it afforded them the joy of doing and saying what they liked.
Spotty, as a good friend should, had informed me of his father's wise offerings, almost inferring that 'He, who walks the heavens', must be of 'Middling' years, seeing as my sainted elder sibling had stated that age should not be mentioned.
I had taken umbrage at first, at the mere suggestion that 'He, who walks the heavens' could be likened to we normal beings.
"Oh no, my boy.", had said Spotty Watson's father,

raising himself from his armchair, just enough to let out a most thunderous of farts. Spotty had beamed in pride, while I stood wide-eyes in applause, forgetful of the heinous gas which now drifted through the confines of the small unkempt sitting-room.
"What I meant was", he continued, seating himself back into his chair, "Your elder, and most wisest of siblings, was too above the norm to have his age bandied about. He is forever in prime, I might add."
On top of this, in continuation, Spotty Watson's father also explained the nature of those 'Aged in Pension', informing me that those in detriment of age had the right to say what they liked and to whom, to be crabby and tactless, as befitted those who had reached such an age.
Oh, impatient mind… My mind whirled in its reasoning, to hurtle my life towards that certain age when I could act in a most profane and crabby way to those of a younger and more thoughtless generation!
"I would love to be at such an advanced age!", I exclaimed.
"It will come to you, young man… As it comes to us all."
Oh, was not this the wisest of men! Was not Spotty Watson's father well seated, just beneath the high honour of 'He, who walks the heavens'?
Once again there came the interruption of an eruption as Spotty Watson's father raised himself to that limited elevation.

I will admit to you all, I had never heard my beloved sibling raise a fart. But I will assure you now, that his would make a most rip-roaring and volcanic sound, to be applauded and approved by all.

This reminds me of a memory when my father, small in his being, had 'Misbehaved himself' (My mother's words, not mine!).
He had been seated in an armchair when, without any explanation, he had emitted the whiniest of farts, squeaking it out as does ice-cream when sucked through a small hole made in the end of an ice-cream cone, a thinnest of ejections.
How I pitied him. Why, both Spotty Watson and I had encouraged ourselves to imitate the boom-sounds of Spotty Watson's father, though not into that maturity of thunder, but getting there.

But I digress from the tale....

"Go outside and shake yourself!", had ejaculated my mother in her horror, watching the shamed man rise and leave the room. That was when, looking at me, she had uttered those words, that he had 'Misbehaved himself'!

Spotty Watson's father had once said, and I quote...
'The past is so full of sunny days that one forgets the winters. And the future is such a hopefully predictive source...But the present? It is neither past nor future

and such a flaming waste of time!'

By this reasoning, he considered that it would be a waste of his time working at present, because he saw no future in it. You have to admit, as I did, Spotty Watson's father had the most educated of minds!

He had this way of explaining things about life which made a certain crazy sense, mostly pointing out the fact that only certain things needed to be studied, so that one became educated in a lighter vein, rather than fill the brain with unnecessary sadness and depressive thought.

For instance, he had once given Spotty and I a lecture about poets. This stemmed from the fact that we were given some homework from school, to read part of a play by Shakespeare and write down our impressions of the said piece.

"Now, you take poetry.", he had begun, continuing, "It's a fact that poets are a sad and depressed bunch. A poet will only draw from memory, sad times. I mean, you take old Willie Wordsworth… 'I wander lonely as a cloud'… Now that depresses you right away, doesn't it?

You see?", explained this educated man. "You'll never find a happy poet. Nor will you find an author with a happy outlook. Writers are naturally lonely and secretive people, who sit alone with their thoughts. The same goes for composers, especially those who write classical music and ballads; it's a fact the music stems from deep within the well of emotions. It's a known fact that the author, the composer and the poet are emotionally unstable, all lonely souls with an inner sense of sadness. Excepting, of course, for the poet who writes limericks… Now, someone who writes limericks… Well that's a different matter… He's full of fun and a happy being".

There you see, is the brilliance of such a mind, that life is fun and one should educate the self in such a fun-fashion.

Spotty Watson's father has the most idyllic of lifestyles, seated in his armchair, making up limericks all day, reading comics and newspapers, as well as goggle-watching the television whenever there was a programme about history or nature, anything which bettered his knowledge… All this between the releasing of gasses… What a marvellous way to exist!

But there is a subject which all young boys must become acquainted with, a subject that I had never heard Spotty Watson's father raise; a subject which only my sainted brother might know of, which would elevate me to a higher rank… Even, dare I think, above the knowledge of Spotty Watson's father… I write about the subject which is most secret, most needed, so that young boys, such as myself, might become a man!

Why do I write these words, dear reader? It is a reminder that what I write is all about my present education, those secrets which my elder sibling deigned to impart in his own good time. This write is of times when, ‘He, who walks the heavens’, would impart knowledge which would stand me in good stead within my future.

CHAPTER TWO.

‘THE SECRETS OF WOMEN.’

My time of learning had begun when ‘He, who walks the heavens’ had noticed my new interest in the Lady Maureen Soap, who lived two doors down.

Prior to my interest in the female form, my time had been taken up with catapults, bows and arrows and other youthful weapons. The Lady Maureen Soap was simply a person, considered to be an adult and of no interest to me at all.

What happened to my mind and thinking, I was not sure. I do know that I had begun to look less at the Cowboys and Indians at the cinema, looking more at the form of the female whom the heroes fought over. These strange urgings and needs, I kept to myself. I am sure my best friend, Spotty Watson, would have been horrified to know that my eyes were turning more and more to ’Girls’!

It began on the Wednesday. ..

I remember it was a beautiful morning and I had stood in front of the house, my eyes glazed in appreciation. I was not aware that ‘He, who walks the heavens’ had stepped out from the front door and now stood beside me.
“What are you up to, young nonity?”, he asked, his large and flawless blue eyes following my gaze, to consider the shape of the Lady Maureen Soap as she graced the road on her way to the bus-stop.

"Ah...I see... the gonads are beginning to droop.", he assumed, a smile lighting his perfect face.

Oh, most wondrous of men, my mind cried out. Such insight is well beyond my reasoning, for I was not sure what this beautiful man did see, or, indeed, what gonads were, but I felt the rise of pride that 'He, who walks the heavens', had noticed the lowering of my gonads.

"I think.", said he, taking my left ear, in not an un-spiteful way and leading me back into the house... "It is time I began to teach you the facts of life, the 'Secrets of Women'... So that you learn to survive the perils of maturity."

I then learned, through these times of instruction, that a ritual had to be followed. It began when 'He, who walks the heavens' seated himself in the back-sitting room, his mind on Angels, while I was dispatched to the kitchen, to make a fresh pot of tea. Upon my return, I was to pour, and place the cup of piping hot tea onto a saucer and then place the said tea into this majestic fellow's hands. Then, upon tasting, he would smack his lips, signifying that I might sit on the coconut matting at his feet. There, I would wait until tea was drunk and the lesson began.

My first lesson was a test of endurance, in that I sat in pose, my thin legs crossed, as were my arms, my eyes upon the beautiful face of 'He, who walks the heavens', waiting with bated breath as he, first, drank his tea, then perused the daily newspapers with such dalliance that I had to keep myself from moving about like a puppet with St. Vitas Dance.

Eventually…

"Thus ends the first lesson.", he said, rising and with a most wondrous sound, stretched out his arms in an effort to ease the tension.

"Excuse me, my lord.", I whispered.

I found it paid me well to speak to this heavenly man in whispers, so that my thin high voice did not offend his ears. Again, the reference to this beautiful person as being a Lord, only befitted his bearing and my subservience.

'He, who walks the heavens' made no answer, although his arched eyebrow indicated that I might continue my speech.

"Excuse me, my lord.", I whispered again. "But what was the lesson about?"

My lord smiled, such a blissful expression that the pain of my creased and folded limbs simply evaporated.

"Patience.", he explained.

I feared to ask more. Patience was a word I was unsure of, though I was now sure that it had something to do with the 'Secrets of Women'.

"Impatience is the curse of youth.", said my sweet

elder sibling, suddenly breaking into my thoughts and sharpening my eyes to his face.
"To even begin to understand the 'Secrets of Women' one has to understand the art of patience."
My ears evaluated each word which came from such ruby lips, hearing them and planting each syllable into my memory-box.
"One cannot expect to pluck the richest cherry from the tree, until it had ripened to a full sense of fruitfulness. One has to learn to wait, until the fruit almost falls into a waiting hand."
Oh, dearest brother, my heart spoke, you who lives among the Angels, are you not the kindest of men, that in such nature you give me time to teach me of patience, to make me realise the 'Impatience of Youth'.
Thus was my agony of impatience explained, that I would have to learn to be patient, to wait until such times as the 'Secrets of Women' was to be revealed. Indeed, in my youth, would I bear the harsh tension of impatience and wait until 'He' decided the time of the 'Telling'.

Mind you, as an aside… I was not sure exactly what cherries and fruit-bearing trees had to do with it. Though I knew, as did all small boys, that the ripest and juiciest of cherries, would salivate any mouth, closing the eyes in pure joy as the mouth tasted the sweetness of a ripe, succulent, cherry.
I was sure, as I imparted to Spotty Watson later, I

would wait all of a lifetime to have my share of a bag of red-ripe cherries!

Waiting is so hard for a young boy. A hour is a lifetime, when the reward is so great. Indeed; time is a deadliest enemy, the arch-enemy of patience. Such a time caused me, once again to stand before Spotty Watson's father. Repeating this importance to Spotty Watson's father, about 'Time', gained me the intelligence that patience and the plucking of a ripe cherry, plus the planting of a seed, would then produce 'The fruit of one's loins'!

Impatience is, indeed, a curse of youth, especially since the 'Urges of maturity' seemed to be moving at a faster rate than my education.
As Spotty Watson's father informed me…
"Without education, one is left to the devices of imagination and colours of impression…And this leads to fear."

Now imagination is something all young boys understand, we live in its world, a world of pirates and heroes, and all young boys know about fear too. It is only those who are strapping in build, like Bully Wilson, whom seemed to lack any sense of fear.
So it was, when Spotty Watson's father opened this conversation with these words, Spotty and I settled ourselves to learn about fear.

"Indeed, fear is such a useful tool for those who make use of its psychology. It's a fact that only the educated and the insane lose any sense of fear. It has to be admitted here, that the mad person is one who has allowed imagination to override the sense of logic, unable to reason the sense of fear… And, in this sense, we can discount the madman."
Spotty Watson's father seemed lost within his thoughts for a time, watery blue eyes in vacant stare, seeming lost on a grey splodge which lived on the ceiling. He scratched absently at his nose, then, becoming aware of a certain need, lifted himself to one side to rid himself of the gasses which had bulged his stomach since breakfast.

I had been lost in my own thoughts, allowing fear to enlarge my imagination, so that I saw demons and furies, which chased my mind with huge scary eyes. Oh, bless my saints… I would seek all kinds of education, if it helped combat such fearsome beasts. The outpour of thunder, which erupted from the rear-end of Spotty Watson's father, brought my mind back to earth.
In my descent to solid ground and reasoning, I could now understand that Bully Wilson was quite mad, the madness being the real reason for his lack of fear. I decided to be more lenient in my thinking, when it came to Bully Wilson.
"If you take the uneducated man.", continued Spotty Watson's father, leaning back into his grubby

armchair, his voice now becoming a whisper of threatened doom…
“And place him into a darkened forest, he will know fear, the noises which seem to come from magic places. He will run in panic and pay any price to stop the demons, the makers of magic from tearing at his soul.”
I felt the hairs rise on the back of my neck, my uneducated mind lost in the dark of the imagined forest. I could hear the demons, feel the aura of magic. I could also see, from the roundness of Spotty Watson’s eyes, that he, too, felt the same imagined fear and, like me, would have paid any price to be saved from this hell.
Spotty Watson’s father lost his demonic look, his face placid in explanation…
“You see, my boys, the educated man would have learned that the noise was only the wind, high up in the trees which caused the sounds, so that imagination would begin to run riot. The educated man would not tell the ignorant fellow the facts of the noise, rather he would paint a more sinister picture, enlivening the fear, until the poor unintelligent man paid good money so his soul might be saved from such imagined devils!”

Now, while this telling had no bearing on the ‘Secrets of Women’, it helped realise the grandness of Spotty Watson’s father’s mind. He was, indeed, next to ‘He, who walks the heavens’, a greatest of minds, even though the intelligence was too clever to be grasped by simple minds such as we, Spotty and I, possessed.

"Now you take education and women.", said this great man.
My ears became swollen, each head-side orifice enlarged to its fullest degree, so that nothing was missed. The very word, 'Women', had sharpened my attention so that I listened intently.
"Now women are strange creatures.", he entertained. "Unlike we men, who are naturally earthed, women are 'Cloud-risen', conducted through emotions and passions, ruled by feelings of romanticisms and strange areas of dreams."
I will admit to you now, dear readers, my mind was awhirl with such thoughts. It was true then, that women lived up there, in the clouds, like Angels! I felt my chest constrict with this knowledge and I took deep, gulping, breaths to bring myself back down to 'Man-trodden' earth.
I nodded my enthusiasm, my eagerness to learn about the inner workings of these mysterious beings. I now fully understood why my own dear father would look in awe whenever my mother demanded a condition. It was not, as I thought, that her bulk intimidated him, that fear made him commit to any act she so demanded…It was because he adored her, as would any man adore an angel!
The 'Teller of Tall Tales' continued…

"Having established this fact, that women are in tune with sweet words and have sweet and romantic tastes… I will continue to demonstrate why it pays to be educated…And why the educated man has the pick of the peaches, the cream of the crop.
The uneducated man will realise that women want to be wooed, need to be romanticised…It has to be known that a woman in love will not count the hours, but will become a domestic goddess all the hours of the day to please the man of her dreams. Thus, a woman has to be wooed, romanticised, as I have said. Now, the uneducated man has only a limited intelligence and will woo a lady with presents, he will try to win affection through the sweet scent and taste of flowers, chocolates and other items. Ergo, my young friends, this tells us that the uneducated man has to work awfully hard to be able to afford the gifts which will arouse the chosen lady's tastes.
Here we come to the important point of this lesson, so listen carefully…"

Had I listened more intently, I am sure I would have fallen from my chair, so intent was I in my listening. My nodding head urged on this magnificent of speakers, this 'Teller of Tall Tales.'

"What the unintelligent man fails to appreciate, my boys, is the fact he has appealed only to the scent and sense of the woman's material tastes. One can eat sweets, smell flowers, wear jewellery and the

like…But the effect soon wears off.
'Today's sweets are tomorrow's needs'…
So the uneducated man has to continue to feed such needs, which, of course means, he has to work all the harder, to afford such gifts. Now, while such trinkets might delight the sense of sight, smell, touch, hearing and taste…It does not fill the area of emotion and passion which a woman needs, so that the cloud of romanticism can be imprinted forever…
On top of which, having eaten such a fill, in time the domestic goddess becomes gorged on such sweetmeats that she cannot continue to perform her duties, caused through the extremities of weight…
Thus domestication suffers in the weight of time!
Listen, my dear young fellows, to any lady and you will hear them say…'It's not the present, it's the thought that counts'.
There now, from their own mouths comes the admission that they need their hearts and minds filled with something which gives them a heart and mind full of passion… And here is the crux!…
The educated man will never buy a present for a woman, he will use his education and intelligence to write the chosen lady a romantic poem…
Words!…Words which fill her heart and soul with passion, a mind which will never forget the words, written on a single sheet of parchment, an original expression of love!…
And that, my boys, is why the educated man never has to pay… Why, like me, he does not have to slog

his heart out, working all those hours, just to pay for sweetmeats that lead to second and third helpings!"

Having spoken for that length of time, Spotty Watson's father sat back and gazed at us fondly, while we, in educated joy, gazed back in open admiration.

"Do you write Mother some romantic poems?", asked Spotty. His father smiled at him, reaching forward to draw him closer.

"By boy", he almost whispered. "I write your Mother a poem every day, a small piece of romantic juice… And I hide it within this very room.".

Spotty and I cast sneaky darting glances around, our eyes searching for any tale-tell sign of scraps of paper.

"Why do you hide it?", questioned Spotty, giving up in his quest to discover any secret place.

"Well, dear boy… It is a game we play. I write the poems and hide them. Your Mother finds them and considers me a most romantic man…And I…?".

We waited with bated breathe, knowing that the end would conclude in a sentence of sheer wisdom.

"And I know that your Mother has used her time on cleaning!".

On finishing this amazing piece of information, Spotty Watson's father rose from his throne and, powered by a series of back-spluttering farts, like a misfiring engine, left the room, and me to my thoughts.

I decided then, I would be the writer of most romantic poems. A sad and lonely soul I might be, but also a dark and mysterious person. Indeed, I was determined to learn. I knew then, that education was the route through life, that I would have women falling at my feet…I would have my very own domestic goddess!… I would never seek out work, instead I would become, like Spotty Watson's father, highly educated and able, too, to produce those wonderful thunder-loud farts which came so easily to him.

"A most wonderfully educated man your father is, Spotty.", I said.
"Indeed, he is.", replied Spotty.

Strange, is it not, how one yearns to be in another place, to own what one cannot have. This was my reflection on the way home. I mean, I come from a good home, or so my mother informs me at every given opportunity. My home is well kitted out, clean and respectable. Yet I loved the freedom and spirit of Spotty Watson's house. I loved the ambience, the tired welcome of the sofa and armchairs which squeaked on seating, the life in the washed-out curtains and the joy of open expression, the joy of letting go a real rip-snorter of wind, without fear of being ostracized from the family home.

Thus was my thinking as I dawdled my way home,

not forgetting to mind the cracks in the paving as I walked. I suppose every schoolboy dawdles, it is their prerogative, to dawdle, to give the mind time to wander and muse…And as for the fear of stepping on the 'Cracks' in the pavements as one walks; here again, every schoolboy knows that doing so was to put life and limb at risk. I do remember a time when Freckles Malloy was once dared to put his life to the test by walking on a crack. Well, not only did he do it once, he did it twice!

I might tell you, dear readers, within two weeks, his whole world was in torment. First Bully Wilson had taken his sweet ration, a whole bagful of sticky toffees, and then he dropped his lead soldier, the one of Napoleon Bonaparte on his horse, down a drain… So there you are, a lesson indeed!

My 'Mind-Musing' and 'Crack-Stepping' was brought to an abrupt halt when I espied the beautiful shape of the Lady Maureen Soap walking down the road towards me.

At an earlier time, during one of my 'Seatings' in the toilet at home, I had been reading a book, wherein it described a man as having…'The Look of Love' about him'. I had tried to find out what this particular look was, and had searched in all the dictionaries in the Library, but to no avail. Being a boy of some determination (Though, judging by my small frame, you might not see this!)… I had decided to find my own 'Look of love.'.

Having borrowed my mother's hand-mirror from her bedroom, I had spent many hours seated on the toilet, perfecting what I considered to be the 'Look of love'.
And now is my final hour, for, with the approach of the fair Lady Maureen Soap, I decided to take fate into my hands and give her my 'Look of love.'

"Are you ill?", she asked, staring at me with some consternation. With that, she pushed past me and hurried on without a backward look. I deduced from that, the Lady Maureen Soap had never seen a person wearing the 'Look of Love'.

Though downhearted and with much thinking to do, I made my way to my front door and knocked.

"Have you been out?".

My father, whom my sainted elder sibling had named 'The Underling', was often in this frame of mind, to state the obvious. I mean, had he not just opened the door to allow me entrance into the family home? Is it not reasonable to deduce that I must have been out, for me to come in?

"Of course he's been out!"

My mother, known to me as 'The Queen', was a large, statuesque woman. Well, that is what I had

heard my father say to Uncle Joseph at one time… "She is statuesque", adding… "A statue, carved with a heart of stone".
Spotty Watson's father had described her as 'Ruebanesque', though I never did find out what the word meant.
"Of course he's been out!", my Mother asserted again, with withering glare.
Then to me, she demanded…
"Where have you been?… I am talking to you…Are you listening?".
Now; it is every young boy's duty to allow his mind to wander, is it not, dear reader? And by the same maxim, is it not every mother's duty to awaken the child's mind to reality?
"Yes, Mother of mine.", I replied in an awakened state, answering her question.
"So? Where have you been?"
Why on earth do parents always ask this question? Do we young people ever ask of our parents where they have been, when they return from some secret business. of course we do not. In fact, there is some sense of pleasure when parents are dismissed from our minds and out of sight. Spotty Watson is the only boy I know who actually likes to be with his father. I will state though, here and now, if I had a parent like Spotty Watson's father, I, too, would want to be near him at all times.
"Speak, boy…Why are you always in dreams?".
"I was at Spotty Watson's house, my mother", I

replied, coming down from dream's domain.
"That spotty little boy? I wish you wouldn't have anything to do with him. He needs to see a dermatologist, he is infected."
My mother had this regal lift to her head, so that, when she talked of someone or something she disliked, eyes descended down the arch of her nose, which contributed, I suppose, to the saying that…'One looks down one's nose.'
"And I wish you would stop talking in that silly way. I am your mother, so stop saying 'My mother' when talking to me!"
"But…Are you not my mother?"
"Don't be smart with me, child. I really think there is something wrong with your brain!"
Behind her, my father nodded assent at my answer, to whit that, indeed, she was my mother. His head still nodded when, in an astonishing turn of speed, my mother spotted her husband in nodding action.
"You are as simple as your son!", she determined, sweeping away in regal tread. My father, in his shame, with downcast eyes, squandered his way into the sitting room and seated himself in an armchair, feeling safer as the sides of the chair swamped his small form.

I was once informed by Spotty Watson's father that, should a parent like your choice of friends, then such friendships should be avoided, because it is not a natural consideration. Boys should have friends who

go against the sensitivity of the parents. It would seem that this is part of the learning towards adulthood, that loyalty for a friend comes before the wishes of the parents (Especially the mother!)… Loyalty and the art of defence against dominance is very important in life.
This was my thinking, that I would remain friends with Spotty Watson till my expiration, I would be loyal and defend his honour so that I might emerge into adulthood as a fit and healthy person and, although fearful, never dominated by my mother, 'The Queen.'

We boys all know how to 'Sidle' and 'Skulk', for we are a secretive lot and often need to creep into a house and up the stairs before any parent could capture and interrogate us, as to our earlier whereabouts. I was very much a 'Sidler', slithering my way up the stairs to my small bedroom at the top of the house.
But I also reasoned it was worth a 'Skulk' as I passed the bedroom of 'He who walks the heavens.' Thus I paused at 'His' door, and skulked, my ear pressed to the wood, my heart racing, for fear this mightiest of all men might suddenly bound out and catch me skulking.
His music played…Oh, joyous sounds of such soothing. 'He who walks the heavens' played soft and sentimental 'Angel Music'. I listened, my hand to my chest, to control and quieten the racing pulse

of my heart.
It is strange how music brings on memories…
I reflected on a time when 'He who walks the heavens' had, in softened mood, once deigned to speak to me about music…

"On this earth, young simpleton.", he had said. "There are five known elements".
This had come about because, earlier, I had the audacity to ask 'He who walks the heavens' if he liked music, He had bid me sit before him, and then began to explain his feelings about music.

"These are.", he had continued, " Earth, Air, Fire, Water… And the most important of them all…Is Music. Music is a natural element which feeds the soul. Music uplifts and expands the nature of man. It can make us happy or sad, proud or disillusioned… Music is a time-piece of memory. Once heard, a piece of music will stop the clock and remind us of that exact time when it is heard again in the future. Music is loved by the world. If music were religion then the world would all praise the same element of life. That, my young simpleton, is my answer to you about music."

Now; I was never exactly sure what 'He who walks the heavens meant about 'Elements', but one thing I was sure of was that his wisdom was infinite and I am sure there will be many books written in his

honour at some stage.
And it was while my mind was rolled back to an earlier time that the laxity of my skulking caused me to knock my head against the bedroom door, so that 'He who walks the heavens' had opened it, beetle-browed in magnificent anger, to clasp my ear and shake it.
"What do you want, 'Camel Dung?"
I adopted my humble pose, watering eyes and a dry washing of hands, openly submitting, my mind fumbling over exaggerated reasons as to why I should be 'Skulking' outside the door of such a holey shrine.
"My Lord.", I whispered through the ear-tugging pain. "I wish to hear more about the 'Secrets of Women'."
Relief was immediate as the ear was released and the beetling of brows was replaced by a most beatific smile.
"Tomorrow, 'Smallest of Turds', I will begin to instruct you in the secret knowledge of women."

Oh, my heart had soared like that of an eagle, uplifted on the enthusiasm of thermal currents… Tomorrow, I would know!

Now, I am neither an intellectually strong boy, nor do I have the outstanding frame or likeness of my elder sibling, 'He who walks the heavens'. This sad fact I bear, so I am reliably informed by my mother, was because I took after my father…Or, as Spotty Watson's father had said, quoting Shakespeare… "The quality of juice was severely strained!".

But the next day it seemed that 'He who walks the heavens' made no attempt to further my intelligence about the 'Secrets', even though I made every possible effort to cross his path at every given chance. It appeared that my sainted elder sibling had forgotten his promise to me, not even stopping to consider my small frame in passing.
And so, I sadly lacked the intelligence as to how I should get, 'He who walks the heavens', to begin to tell me the truth about the 'Secrets of Women'. I mean, there is no way one might dare infringe of this magnificent fellow's time or try his patience. I could not just walk up and ask my elder sibling to tell me about the 'Secrets'. Indeed, such a demand would get me a disapproving glare or, at worst, a smart clip to the ear. This sad fact, this lack of information had caused my face to wear quite a downcast look.

" I'm sure my father will have an idea as to how to get your elder sibling to open up.", said Spotty Watson, on hearing my reason for wearing such a downcast mask.
So it was, that I eventually sought the answer from that most educated of men, the 'Teller of Tall Tales'.

"And so, Sir… How would you suggest I ask 'He

who walks the heavens' to tell me the secret?".
Spotty Watson's father scratched at his nose.
"Man.", he said, " Survives on a diet of stuffed ego and the wine of vanity."
I nodded my appreciation at these words. There was something dramatic and deep about them, I was not fully aware of what they meant, but the silence which followed had such a loudness of appeal that I remained in awed silence, saying nothing, savouring the thoughts of ego and vanity. My mind was so lost in this, that I almost missed the further explanation.
"Reverse psychology.", came the explanation.
"Pardon?…Reverse psychology, Sir", I echoed.
"Indeed, my boy…. Starve the ego and empty vanity's flask.".
Spotty Watson stood at his father's side like some adoring slave boy, or Siamese prince I had seen in the film version of 'The King and I'. He stood upright, an arm resting lightly on the headrest of the armchair, a most regal pose indeed, not even moving in the slightest when a 'Gianormously' ripping fart almost parted his hair.
"Beans", explained the 'Teller of Tall Tales', as he regained composure.
"The ego and the flask, Sir.", I prompted.
"Ah…Yes… Let me see."
There was a pause while Spotty Watson's father searched his memory, eyes raised to the ceiling, a quick nose-pick and then…
"Yes, I remember… Now, young fellow, there are

two methods of action, which I shall call plan 'A' and plan 'B'. The first, plan 'A' is to out-wait your elder sibling…"

"But I have been doing so, Sir… Indeed, I have been the very virtue of patience…".

My voice trailed off as I realised that Spotty Watson was looking at me in a most unkind way, making me realise that I had overstepped the mark by interrupting the 'Teller of tall Tales' during his education.

"I am sorry, Sir.", I said, the contrition bringing tears to my eyes.

Spotty Watson nodded approvingly while his father, graciously accepting my apology with a wave of the hand, continued…

"Then… Be patient just a while longer and, should the waiting become so uncomfortable that it brings on depression, you set about gaining your sainted brother's attention by attacking with 'Plan B', his masculinity. Mind you, one has to be very subtle while doing this, because your elder sibling is a very proud man and quick to antagonise, most certainly when you question his virility, which will deflate his ego.".

I really was lost in this maze of words, and rather dubious about attacking the virility of 'He who walks the heavens'. I might not know exactly what 'Virility' was, but I did know that my sainted elder sibling could land a hefty hit which would leave loud bells ringing in the head for some time.

“Then what do I do, Sir?”, I begged
Drawing me closer to him, Spotty Watson’s father began to explain just how subtle I should be in testing the virility and ego of my elder sibling.
I listened intently to the plan, both excited and fearful, but determined to put this plan into action as soon as possible.

It was on the Thursday afternoon that I found a most perfect time. ‘Plan A’, the time of waiting patiently had expired into hours of depressive thought, so it was time for ‘Plan B’ to be put into action.

‘He who walks the heavens’ was seated in his favourite chair, savouring the newspaper gossip, one foot delicately placed across one knee as all gentlemen do.
In furtive fashion, I sidled past the door, not once but twice, to work up the courage for this assault.

Now; as I had stated earlier, I was never a strong boy, neither, according to ‘He, who walks the heavens’, intellectually strong, or as a physical specimen. But there were times when I just had to summon up the courage and strength to question this ‘Sainted Giant’ Courage gained, I entered the room and knelt before him.

"Why.", I had asked with trembling shake, "Do you not have a girlfriend, my Lord?".

My brother has risen from his chair, giving me such a withering glare that I tried hard to bury myself into the coconut matting beneath my small frame. Suddenly; he relaxed and with a smile which worried me, 'He who walks the heavens', regained his seat before quickly reaching out to grasp me by the front of my shirt so that my eyes bulged and my throat rattled out fearful sounds.

"You smallest of vermin, utterance of diseases."

His voice, in full magnificence, displayed its anger, so that I feared I had completely destroyed his virility, starved his ego and emptied his flask of vanity of all total contents! Suddenly, he let go his grip so that I tumbled back, terrified now at the whiteness of my sainted elder siblings cheeks.

"Forgive me, my Lord!", I begged, bowing so low that my nose dipped hard into the matting

"How dare you be so impertinent, you scrapings of a Dung-Beetle!".

Yes, I would admit, I was those things he called me. How dare I, a Dung-Beetle's last scrapings, have the audacity to question such a power.

"But I only wanted you to tell me about the 'Secrets of Women', my Lord.", I wept.

Perhaps my tears and the begging attitude I posed, head dipped low while my hands reached up in supplication, touched my elder siblings heart. He lifted me up, a sympathetic smile beautifying those perfect features.

"Sit, small person and listen.", he commanded.

Now, thoroughly ashamed by my attempt to empty the strengths of this sainted man's ego, I straightened and composed myself, cross-legged, as we do in the 'Cubs' at a meet.

"Why do I not have a girl?".

It was not so much a question aimed at me, rather a musing aimed high as he gazed upward in thought.

"I do not have a girlfriend, 'Brain smaller than a knat's testical', because I have girlfriends....With an S!".

Oh, the elation, the sacrifice of my offence was well worth the answer! My sainted brother had not let me down! There was no doubt this handsomest of all men had hundreds of women who worshiped him, who lay at his feet as Mary Magdalene had in that picture of Christ, my mother kept over her bed....(The one I once caught my small wizened father secretly laughing at!).

"Let me tell you about women, 'Small sacrificial object'. Let me put you wise about the female and their upbringing."

‘Oh my brother’, my mind wept… ‘Lead me on to a higher glory, I pray thee.’ He was my hymn, my soul-inspired guide in all matters of female mysticism. I sat, enthralled as he spoke, my eyes alive in concentration. I was about to learn the ‘Secrets of Women’.

"There are laws which all young girls have to learn from their mothers. They are secret laws, handed down by word of mouth from mother to daughter from time immemorial.".

My God! So that delicious creature next door, Lady Maureen Soap, the young siren of the street who wore soft white knickers... (I had seen them on next doors washing-line once and had even climbed the brick wall to reach and touch the soft, velvet, material.)... She was under such secret instruction from her mother! Small wonder she barely glanced at me when I stared with longing eyes at her lithe figure as she made her way down the street.

"Are you listening, ‘Droppings of excreta’?".

I startled myself to attention as his toe tapped a smart thump to my knee.

"Now… I shall tell you some of the secrets taught to young girls as is the custom. Tell me this...Have you ever seen a married man with a happy face?".

Now, I must admit here and now, that I had not. My father had a constant and fearful expression whenever he entered the house, mournful and subjective. Thinking on it; even Spotty Watson's father, in married state, seemed to have little to smile about. It was indeed true... Married men had very little pleasure in their lives. I shook my head in affirmation.... (I wondered on that afterwards; how can someone gesture non-affirmation by ascertaining agreement!)...My brother had left me behind and I chased my mind to catch up.

"Girls are taught simple basic rules to follow once having captured a poor soul of a mate.... And listen on, 'Worm who crawls'...", added the fount of all wisdom, waving a large finger into my face... "These are the simple facts."

Here 'He who walks he heavens' leaned closer and near whispered in conspiratorial tone…

"A girl is taught, first, that a boy has to get rid of his friends once a relationship has started. No more 'Boys' Nights' Out'! There are other young, single, girls who gather in tribal groups, waiting to pounce on the weaker boys who stray from the strength of the pack. And so, it is imperative that the girl divorces her beau from his friends, thus controlling his movements and away from such local haunts, the watering-holes, wherein the female packs hunt.

Once this is established, the boy reduced to a mere lonely shadow, the next part of the operation comes into force... To meet up with and make eternal friends with, the boys' mother. Now this bonding is very important, it is the binding force which then separates the young lady from her own mother as the new, soon to be 'Mother-In-Law' takes over the reigns. That, my young 'Turd of a camel', is why they are called 'Mothers-In-Law'; because they are the ones who make sure that all family laws are obeyed."

I gasped in my understanding. Oh, my giddy aunt! So that was why my small wizened father used to hide when Nanny came to visit, why mother and 'Mothers' mother' vanished into the secret confines of the kitchen and were not to be disturbed. Father had called them gossips but now I had the truth of it all.

Oh wise, superior being of a brother...You open my eyes to such mysteries!

I gazed up at this 'Golden Lord', my eyes urging him ever on, to divulge more of these secrets, these matriarchal machinations. 'He, who walks the heavens' smiled, then continued…

"I might inform you, 'All species of turd', that the future Mother-In-Law will secretly inform the newly allied girlfriend of all the necessary news she needs to know... How much the lad earns and his future prospects...His habits, good and bad...In what areas of life he needs to be trained and what other young ladies had entered his life prior to this recent engagement. The instruction is endless, until the girl has every scrap of information needed to psychologically reduce the boy to a pulp.

And the most important lessons are so secret that even I, who knows all, have not yet been allowed to learn....The sexual attitude.".

I had been somewhat confused for a short while, simply because this wise, this most righteous of leaders seemed uninformed about the full scriptures of the 'Secrets of Women'. But his sudden warm and sunny smile, which lightened up the whole magnificence of his noble face, gave me warning that he had some information to impart on the subject.

"I have to get ready to go out now, small insignificance.", he said, suddenly rising and stretching to full height, stepping over me as one steps over a small whipped dog.

I was left, uninformed, subdued, perplexed and bitterly disappointed by his leaving...But I knew that 'His Holiness', in all his majesty, would be back to complete this magnificent 'Telling of secrets'!

It seemed as if half my life had passed me by as I waited for 'He who walks the heavens' to finish the most important part of the 'Telling'. My continual soundings of 'Tuts and Sighs' seemed to have no effect on his nerves. It seemed I was invisible, a 'Nonity', to be treated with complete indifference by 'My Lord'… Until…

I had risen early on the Saturday morning, escaping from captivity, about to run so that I could meet up with Spotty Watson. We had planned to visit a museum uptown, which invited this early-morning start. I was about to creep from the house, gently easing the front door closed, when I saw, further down the street, acting in a very furtive manner, my sainted elder sibling. He was coming out of the Lady Maureen Soap's house!

Oh, my giddy aunt! My mother would be so displeased to know that her most adored son had made friends with a 'Commoner' like the Lady Maureen Soap!

What marvelous information I had…

Now; there is in me a sneak of sorts, there must be, simply because I was aware this information would be of use to me in a sneaky way.

Having returned from my visit with Spotty Watson to the museum, I waited until I 'Happened' to chance a meeting with my most sainted elder sibling.

"I see the lady Maureen Soap has caught your eye, my giant brother.", said I with a whisper.

The fact I had seen him creeping out from the fair lady's house was neither here nor there. There was no need to mention my Mother… It was enough he understood that I knew...

Later, I would pray for my sneaky nature.

“What do you want, you disgusting child?”.

“I wondered, my lord, if you had time to tell me the rest of the ‘Secrets of women’.”

My brother, in his mightiness, deigned to further my knowledge about the secrets of women, and, seating me before him with a thump, scratched at his neck as he sat, throne-wise, in thought.

"Now where was I, smallest of blackmailers?", he pondered.

The fact that I, the insignificant 'Nonity' was now risen in estimation, since ‘He, who walks the heavens’, has infered a new name on me. I am now called...'Blackmailer!' Oh, wondrous name! Later I would seek out the meaning of this word.

"You told me about the girl who, having now trapped her beau, is instructed by the Mother-in-Law in the ways of causing eternal unhappiness, as does our father suffers in his marital grief."

"Ah...Yes...I have it now."

Oh the joy! ‘His Mightiness’ had actually touched my shoulder gently with a sacrificial tenderness. I am risen in a further estimation!

"We shall return to the times of the Ancient Greeks, then.".

My mind whirled at this prospect, for I had, at an earlier seating, learned from this majestic being, my brother, that all goodness had derived from this ancient brotherhood. O happy acquiescence!

"At this time, ‘Droppings of a camel’, there lived a man named Aristophanes. And it was he, a noble poet and playwright who found out the secret of the most devious of women's whiles."

Oh, may the Lord enlarge my ears, that I might hear all. May this magnificent man be praised, for this service ‘He of all knowledge’ does me!

"In his play, The Lysistrata, it is explained that, when a woman wants something which the husband, by his right, refuses to give, the woman then uses a most devious and secretive method, whereby the husband, in his weakness will act contrary to his nature by giving in.".

My eyes were open wide in anticipation, my heart throbbing with excitement.

" This spell performed on the strongest of men is given in one reoccurring sentence...This sentence is the bane of all manhood and reduces the strongest ‘Hercules’ to a shriveled-up weed.".

My breath wheezed out from me in dread anticipation..

"The sentence?", I whispered....

‘He who imparts all wisdom’ rose high, like a dark avenger and strode from the room, after saying... "Not tonight, dear...I have a headache!"

CHAPTER THREE.

'ON WOOD AND WOMEN.'

"Youth.", said Spotty Watson's father. "Has a most efficient way of overcoming disappointment."

I was seated on the floor, alongside Spotty, staring up at Spotty Watson's father, who spent some time, searching his teeth with a tongue and finger, reaching in for scraps of food which had secreted itself there after lunch. His tongue, suddenly rested its exploration while a finger-nail raked in and extracted an offending particle. Holding a stubby finger up to the light, Spotty Watson's father examined the nuisance.

"A tomato pip!", he exclaimed, giving the seed a deft flick which whirled it away at an excited speed.

Spotty and I exchanged glances, very aware of the dangers of swallowed seeds. A while ago, left to our own devices, so that we 'Mooched' through my home in a slow wander. It happened that, as we 'Mooched' through the empty home, we came across a large bowl of fruit, a table centre-piece in the lounge. It is well known that young boys have a very large appetite, aided by a large open gullet which (According to Spotty Watson's father…) was because young boys had not yet grown an 'Adam's Apple', which acted as a sort of 'Gob-Stopper', affording a more delicate swallow.

But…I digress… To continue…

In effect, Spotty and I relieved the bowl of two large and rosy apples, taking our booty down to the shed at the bottom of the garden. There, we devoured the said apples, our eyes closed in the salivating joy of such a sweet taste. It is known that boys are 'Dustbins'. This was my mother's description, claiming that boys will eat everything and anything. In truth, this is a fact, in that Spotty and I ate the apples, cores, stalks and all.

It was only after the eating that I considered the fact that an apple tree grew from a single pip, the seed wild in growth if the weather was heated. This conversation ended when it was feared that the apple seeds we had swallowed would bear fruit, as it were, the heat within causing the seeds to sprout and grow within our bodies, so that the branches would erupt and extend from every orifice our bodies offered. Such fear and imagined effect caused us to rush up to the bathroom, whereby, with fingers jammed down our throats, we regurgitated the apples, seeds, stalks and whatever else we had filled our stomachs with during the morning.

These 'memory-actions' of an earlier time lost me part of what Spotty Watson's father was saying, about how youth overcame disappointment. I wish I had been more attentive, because I was still tasting the disappointment of not having the 'Secrets of Women' properly finalized by 'He who walks the heavens'. And, right now, here was a further disappointment, that I had missed the escape route from this depressed sense.

It was at this time that Spotty Watson's mother made an appearance, 'Slippering' in from the kitchen to stand before her husband. She wore a headscarf and pinafore dress, in the same way as did my mother's cleaner, that 'Mrs. Mops woman', as my mother called her. I liked Spotty Watson's mother. She was not beautiful, having lost out to age, but her eyes held a kind of pale blue sadness which I found attractive.

"More tea, Watson?".

"No more. Watson."

Before confusion sets in, I might explain that this short conversation between Spotty Watson's parents was quite normal to them. They called each other by their surname. 'A term of endearment', had explained Spotty Watson when I had first heard this strange calling. Spotty had also gone on to explain his father had also told him that 'Terms of endearment' might only be used after a length of time which was what 'Real love' really was.

"Love.", had furthered Spotty. "Comes after a long period of association. It is an affection of custom, as one sees it as customary to find an armchair in a position it has always been. Should one remove the armchair and it is noticed immediately; but while it stays, in situ, it gives a sense of security."

I will admit, there are times when such references, which Spotty passed onto me from his father's excellent mind, were rather beyond me. To have 'Love' explained as an armchair seemed somewhat strange. But then, this proved how shallow and uninformed my young mind was.

Such was my mind, in past considerations, that it had to fly in fast-forward mode, to realize that Spotty Watson's mother had retreated back into her kitchen and was now, from the sounds of it, busy washing cutlery and humming a tune in quiet happiness. Still humming quietly, she 'Slippered' out from the kitchen and crept her way up the stairs.

Now there were rumblings and a threatening build-up coming from the stomach of Spotty Watson's father. giving warning of a coming eruption. Spotty and I waited with bated breath. The rumblings seemed to spite themselves in an intense way, bubbling and gurgling, then, to our joy, Spotty Watson's father raised himself, to emit a most fearsome noise. It began in a sinister and quiet way, 'Eeking' itself out, then roaring in full throttle as the sound exploded into a volcanic outpouring which startled me so that I jumped to my feet, causing Spotty Watson to follow my example, our eyes ever widening in fright. Fear will always extend the element of time, so that the noise, ever louder, seemed to blast itself into an eternity. Time seemed frozen as Spotty Watson's father, his face set in some kind of grim determination to rid himself of the last essence of methane, grimaced so that one eye closed while the other opened to fullest extent, bulbous and red-veined, till, like the last expiring sounds of a storm, the noise abated in stages, then stopped. Spotty Watson's father seated himself, drawing in deep breaths as he did so, his eyes apportioning themselves to a natural state. He motioned us to be reseated and pointed a stabbing finger out and up, towards the bedrooms. In the ensuing silence came the faint sounds of a vacuum cleaner at work.

"Do you know what that noise is?"

Both Spotty Watson and I remained silent. Obviously, we knew it was the sound of a cleaner at work, but Spotty Watson's father was never obvious in his questions and answers.

"That noise, my boys, is the sound of a 'Happy Woman'."

Both Spotty and I held our silence, listening, with upward-staring eyes to where the sound came from.

"Now I shall tell you something.", said Spotty Watson's father, his voice in lowered fashion so that we leaned forward.

"A busy woman is a 'Happy Woman'."

There, it was out! Spotty Watson's father seated himself back and beamed at us with a huge smile.

It is strange how, when one smiles, another will follow that example, whether one is happy or not. And, to follow that example, both Spotty Watson and I returned the smile in wide reflection.

"Do you know why I say that, my boys?"

Indeed, we did not, for our heads shook in unison, our mouths now losing their smiles. 'TheTteller of Tall Tales' settled himself firmly in his chair, fingertips and thumbs touching, forming an arch.

"I will tell you, my boys…And this is a lesson for you both to carry with you into your future.".

Our nodding heads assured him that his words would be honorably conveyed with us into the far-distant future.

" I tell you both… A woman with time on her hands would have time to think, to ponder, to question and search. A woman in laze would begin to question a man's every move, to question themselves as to why a man had started using after-shave, wearing it for work…And why has he started buying underpants in the latest fashion, spending more and more time in front of a mirror… He had never done all these things before. Such questions were the beginning of the end to extra-marital relationships for any man once a woman had time on their hands to think."

Spotty Watson's father collapsed his 'Finger-Tent', more alive with information.

"Keep them happy, keep them busy.", he advised darkly… "Otherwise a woman has time to ponder and question; to search through personal drawers which she would normally, in a busier frame of mind, simply tuck, fold and stack away without a thought of making unwanted discoveries.".

Settling himself once more, Spotty Watson's father concluded… " Thus, is created the adage that...'A busy woman is a.....'Happy Woman'!"

This information sorted itself, then locked itself into a closed vault within my 'Memory-Bank'. I decided that, should I ever marry in my future, I would be very sure to keep the woman in continual work, therefore keeping her extremely happy!

"Indeed, my boys… As you grow and mature, you will discover that women are a strange breed, with strange fancies…"

'The Teller of Tall Tales' stopped talking as his wife, descending the stairs, carrying a large basket of dirty washing, entered the room and moved into the kitchen. The hum of a washing machine droned in the distance.

"Tea, Watson?"

She had re-entered the room and stood by the doorway, her sad eyes on her partner.

"Not yet, Watson", answered Spotty Watson's father, then, as an afterthought, he said… "In a while… Tell me, Watson; are you happy?".

"Yes… Why do you ask?"

"No reason, Watson, just asking…"

Mrs. Watson gave a sad smile and returned to the kitchen. She began to hum. Spotty Watson's father looked at us in confidence.

"You see lads… A busy woman is a 'Happy' woman!", he said.

With that, Spotty Watson's father lay his head back against the headrest and closed his eyes and, seemingly, within seconds, had started to snore. Spotty Watson rose to his feet, indicating we must leave this man of such high intelligence, to recuperate from his mental distributions. It was as we were about to depart, in soft tread, that he suddenly opened his eyes and said…"Now here's a fact… If a man has a fancy for his wife's best friend, what does he do?"

By the door, Spotty and I turned to look at this great man who, now, seemed wide awake. I marveled at his recuperative powers. What wonder is this, that a man needs only seconds, no, millionths of a second to strengthen a mind which had almost exhausted itself through an effort of educating our young minds. Spotty touched my arm and, together, we regained our seating on the floor in front of this 'Master'. We waited as 'The Teller of Tall tales' stretched his legs out, before picking his nose and inspecting the findings. I knew, as do all small boys, that 'Bogie Duty' was an area all lads understood, though I must confess, I had never seen 'He who walks the heavens' pick his nose. Mostly, I suspect, due to the fact that my sainted elder sibling had a nose of pure cleanliness, nasal passages of a most scented air!

And so we waited, our eyes firmly fixed on the 'Master'.

Although my body was beginning to ache from this sitting posture, I dare not move. These 'Secrets' about women were worth a hundred knives piercing the skin. I would lay quietly on a bed of nails, so that I might hear this most intelligent of men divulge such facts. It is also a fact that we boys are on this earth to learn; and it is more than a fact that Spotty Watson and I were extraordinary lucky to have such a teacher as 'The Teller of Tall Tales'. I went one even better, in that I had the added gift of having an elder sibling who could teach a whole world the truth about these strange and mysterious species, the intricacies of women! With this in mind, I sat still, my eyes in earnest appeal, urging this great man ever onwards. Suddenly, he exclaimed…

"If a man fancies his wife's best friend, he tells his wife!"

I heard the intake of breathe which came from Spotty Watson beside me and must admit, I was astounded at the audaciousness this information proposed. This was akin to daring to ruffle the perfection of golden curls which adorned my elder sibling's head, paramount to committing suicide! But Spotty and I, whatever our thoughts, held our piece, allowing this great mind to explain the wisdom of offering the body to a grave.

"Now, to many, this might seem to have its advantage and a disadvantage… The advantage being that a wife would immediately cast her partner out, so one could continue a life of complete abandonment and debauchery. While… The disadvantage being that the wife, if Amazon-like in stature, would instantly kill you!"

I giggled, due not to a nervous reaction from Spotty Watson's father's words, but rather to the mischievous thought which parked itself on my mind. In my mind's eye, I saw my father, in a meek grace, telling my mother of his fancy for her very best friend, Martha Evergreen-Stokes. The thought enthused itself in expansion, until I realized a picture of my mother, the size of a large barrage balloon, balanced atop the wardrobe, her eyes glaring down on her weed of a husband as he lay on his back on the bed. This mind-action continued, a flash in time, but seemingly slow as my mother, in a terrifying scream of rage, took off in a spread-eagled belly-flop, to completely flatten my father.

This delightful thought was evaporated as Spotty Watson's father, his voice raised to smother my giggle, reiterated…

"He tells his wife! And would the wife throw her partner out, or kill him?... No, she would do neither!", he enthused.

He continued…

"She would tell her very best friend of the husband's reasoning, of his fancy. And here, I shall tell you why, my boys. The wife, you see, always sees her partner as used and worthless...He who passes wind under the blankets, who picks his nose at the dinner-table. She has seen his paunch, his bald patch, the scratch of backside which is every woman's nightmare. Thus she has no fear of imparting such knowledge to her very best friend... And the information that this sad sack of useless unoriginality has a fancy brings both the wife and her friend to fits of helpless laughter."

I, in my simple youthfulness, reasoned this to be a correct assumption. I could never envisage my mother's very best friend, Martha Evergreen Stokes, being attracted to my father, no matter what the condition!

But my assumption was short-lived, because, leaning forward, with a gleam in his eye, Spotty Watson's father imparted the conclusion…

"You see.", he concluded... "Women are a strange breed. Once one becomes aware that they are the condition of a mans' interest, their whole life takes on a new meaning and they see their best friend's husband with new and amorous eyes! And then, my boys... The fun begins!"

Now; while Spotty Watson's father spoke with an authority about women, I needed a more in-depth education, concerning their inner strengths. I mean, it was good to know that a busy woman would be eternally happy and grateful for such loving employment, and to know that women would be quite receptive to the knowledge that a friend's husband had a fancy for her… Such information would enlighten my future time, when a wife's happiness and extra-marital relationships became the norm. But it did not secure me the blessed 'Secrets of Women' I need at this time of urgency!

And so it was that my eyes turned, once more to the knowledge held by 'He who walks the heavens'.

And so, as is my nature, seemingly indifferent, while beneath, there lurked the craftiness of a fox.
I had seen my sainted elder sibling wander his frame down to his favourite chair and, in a fox-like way I wandered into the same room.
"Oh.", I said, in startled concern… " I did not know you were in here, my Lord."
"What do you want, 'Spermatic insect'?"
"Nothing, my Lord., except to please you."
I had dropped my voice to the lisping whisper my elder sibling seemed to enjoy.
"If you wish to please me, 'Dung-Beetle', you may run down to the shop and buy me today's newspaper."
"Perhaps, my Lord, on my return, you might find the good grace to acquaint me more about the 'Secrets of Women".
'He, who walks the heavens' studied me for a longest time, the blue of his eyes seeming to be akin to pools of turquoise liquid.
"Yes, 'Essence of armpits', I shall tell you more, though I will not have you lazing around while I give you knowledge which took me a world of time to gain."
"I will do anything you ask, my Lord…Anything."

‘He, who walks the heavens’ moved his dear mouth in a very thoughtful way, seemingly undecided. Then…

“I’ll tell you what, ‘Small insignificance’. You run and get me a newspaper and, upon your return, you may polish my shoes as I tell you more about the ‘Secrets of Women’. Do we have a deal?”

“Oh, indeed, my Lord.”, I said, moving my frame in speed towards the door.

I had run all the way to the newsagents, paying from my own pocket for the paper and now huffed and puffed as I polished my sainted elder sibling’s shoes. I watched and waited as he rustled the paper before turning each page, studious in reading. I spat on the polish as I had seen my father do and was rewarded by a stern unappreciative glare given to me by my dear brother and, wiping the spittle from the toe-caps with my sleeve, I kept my eyes glued to the work in hand. My huffing and puffing seemed to have little effect on ‘He who walks the heavens’, till, in an exasperated voice which rose above the normal whisper, I asked… "What about the women… Errr… Ladies?", remembering in time that I had earlier been instructed always to call women 'Ladies'... "Bit of respect, is all.", ‘He who walks the heavens’ had advised me.

The paper rustled so that I looked up in quick expectancy.

Then…

"Heat.".

Heat? My brother had uttered that one word and, to me, it was the philosophy of Socrates, the wisdom of Solomon.
"Heat.", he said again and this time looked up from the paper… "Shall I tell you something?"
My mind spiraled upwards and out in a delirium of words, proposing that 'He, who walks the heavens' should inform me of all the mysticisms which a woman holds in secret from we normal men… Oh, speak, my sainted brother, sweeten my ears with your voice, those honeyed tones which carry such delightful information…
Instead, I simply whispered…"Yes please.".
I would listen and stopped in my work as he looked ceiling-wards.
"Women are like wood."
"Wood?", I uttered in awed whisper.
"Yes, 'Undersized sibling', you of tight testicles and high voice."
"Wood."
I half-whispered the words to myself.
Indeed; should you half-whisper this word, 'Wood', to yourself, you would feel a strange sense of magic, a sense of atmosphere one might gain when seated in church, closing the eyes and calling on God.
"Wood", I half-whispered again.
"Where, tell me 'Idiot half-pint', do trees come from?".

This question, directed at me by my sainted brother, brought my mind to a strict concentration. 'He who walks the heavens' had little time for ignorance and would be quite abrupt in dismissal if another seemed not to be listening.
"Forests.", I answered quickly, more in speed and hope than in knowledge.
There was a disdainful grunt of annoyance. I kept my eyes down.
"I meant from which countries, stupid boy".
I continued to polish the shoes, small circles to the toe-caps, eyes downcast, my posture proving my shame of ignorance.
"You will notice that all your trees which come from cold countries, like Norway and even Scotland, are all spruces and firs...", said this sainted man, seeming to forgive my foolishness. And for some idiotic reason, my mouth spoke what my brain thought…
"Yes! Robert The Spruce…He came from....", my voice had trailed off into a darkening silence as 'He who walks the heavens', pearl of all wisdom, glowered with eyebrows drawn in perfect unison which darkened the scowl even more.
"Finished?".
"Yes...I'm sorry.".
My brother accepted my pitiful apology with grand grace, easing himself back into the chair and motioned me on with my shoe-cleaning employment.

"You will understand, small part of my nose-cleaned handkerchief, that all your soft woods come from cold countries.".
I stopped to nod in understanding.
"Now.", continued this wonderful man. "If all the soft woods come from cold climates... What can we deduce from that?".
My brain worked hard but fear retained the answer. I shook my head.
"No. I somehow suspected you would not know, ‘Small insignificance’.", said my noble Lord, before continuing...
"If all cold countries produce soft woods, then it is right to deduce that all hard woods, like Teak and Ebony come from hot countries...Like India and Africa.".
Oh, such knowledge. I would raise my cap to this master, if I wore such a thing. But, then again; this knowledge, though gratefully received and would, no doubt, serve me well in my future, I could not fathom any idea as to how species of wood, whether soft or hard, would give any decent instruction on the ‘Secrets of Women’.

"Now your Ladies also are developed like that.", said this ‘Grand Master’.
Like wood? Grown from trees? Oh, I wanted so much to ask but a wise head held me from questioning.

"Now, 'Underling of our fathers' loins, runt of all litters', what difference is there between soft and hard woods?".
I refused to answer, simply because I did not know.
"The difference lies in the grain, 'Small Pus'. The harder the wood, the closer the grain."
I nodded quickly, as if I had known all along.
"Now.", came the continuation. "The closeness of grain gives more strength. Ergo, hardwoods are stronger than softwoods.".
My sainted brother, bloated in wisdom sat back and held out his feet so that I presented a shoe to each foot, pushing them home in suitable fit.
There was an extended silence as 'He who walks the heavens' examined each shoe, lifting each foot in turn and 'Mooing' his mouth under this inspection.
At last, in satisfied grunt, my sainted elder sibling pushed himself back into the chair, his strong arms stretched out in yawning state.

"Women...Errr....Ladies?", I urged, after a length of time, and fearful that my Lord had forgotten his teaching. I kept my eyes averted. I had learned that direct contact might seem to be something of a challenge, when it comes to manliness. I had no wish to challenge the authority of such a 'Magnificence'.
The creaking of the chair caused me to raise my eyes. 'He who walks the heavens' was now leaning towards me. I waited with bated breathe for him to speak.

"Tea, 'Camel Dung.", commanded his 'Lordship' and I, in dutiful silence made my way out to the kitchen.

'Wood?'

The mind worried itself as the kettle boiled. I tried not to watch it, for we all know what a watched kettle does not!

'Women... Mmmm... Wood and women.'

With tea made, I hurried in with the steaming cup. 'He of all wisdom' had started on a crossword puzzle, frowning, pen between teeth. I sat on the floor nearby, my eyes soft upon his noble face. I knew better than to disturb this handsomest and wisest of all men. I waited for the second part of this 'Telling'.

Like all good things, the second part of this tale was worth the wait. My brother, he of the encyclopedic mind, had kept me in lively suspense, waiting for this finish of his tale about the delights of womanhood.
Meanwhile; and I confess this now, I had found a new love in my life which had, not only my curiosity aroused, but my very whole being. I had found that part of my anatomy, a peculiar extremity, which had another purpose than for just a passing relief. And it

was during one joyous occasion that ‘He who walks the heavens’, chanced upon me as I enjoyed such self-love.
"What are you doing, ‘Weed of the garden’?" he enquired, his eyes firmly centered on the thing I held in my hand.
"Nothing.", I said defensively.

I remember at one time, in an enthusiasm of philosophical reasoning, Spotty Watson’s father had spoken about ‘Defensive/Aggressive’ action…
“When one thinks on it.”, he had said. “A man will become aggressive, defending himself when caught in an embarrassing situation, especially when it concerns any element of manhood. It was not that I became aggressive, for that would gain me some hard and fast retaliation. In this confrontation, I simply became defensive.

"Ah, bless my soul... So you've found your Winkle!". So that was what this marvelous piece of equipment was called!
"More like a ‘Pimple’ than a ‘Winkle.", my sainted brother commented with some distaste as I buttoned-up the waned object.
"You know you can go blind, doing that?", he added.

No, I did not know that, but from that day hence, I would pay particular attention to all those who, with white sticks, tapped their merry way through our squalid streets.

"Plus.", had said my knowledgeable brother. "You lose all your strength. It weakens the spirit, you see.".

Here again, I did not see but listened to his extreme explanation and decided to accept his offer of a business relationship. It was established that I, as junior partner, would do my older and much wiser brothers' bidding, bend to his every whim, for which I was to be given the exact sum of money which would buy me one small bottle of milk and a bar of chocolate each day. It was explained to me that, with such strength-given aid, I might extend the warm hand of friendship to my small 'Winkle' at any time of fancy. I will say, at that time, this was extraordinary handsome of 'He who walks the heavens'.

Now; where was I?...Oh, yes...My brother had made me wait a whole week, until I promised to forgo payment in return for the end to his story about the magic of the female species. I would admit that it was hard, keeping my hands away from the untouchable except in times of toilet-pressure; but I managed.

"Now, 'Twerp of our fathers' loins'.", said my brother as he seated himself and I had squatted down before him. "Let me continue on this tale of the wood and ladies." He held a large hand up before I

could open my mouth. "If you utter one sound, ‘Pimple-Winkle’, our deal is off... Understood?!” Now; how was I supposed to answer without utterance. Oh, sweet brother of mine, in your wisdom you saved me from a savage fate when you continued without waiting for an answer.
"We have established that soft woods come from cold countries and hard woods, reversely, come from hot, have we not?".
I nodded a wise head.
"Soft wood is long grained. It is pliable and easily bent into fashion, you can easily make things from Deal or Pine.".
Here; ‘He, who walks the heavens’ shaped the female form with his hands and I watched, mesmerized, as my wise nodding head asserted wisdom.
"But your hard woods are not so easy to work with. They are short-grained and needing sharp cutting tools, with honed edges to fashion them.".
Now; while this was all very interesting to a Carpenter… (Plus the fact that my sainted brother had omitted to mention that cold climates such as ours produced the hardy Oak alongside others.)… This was not giving much time to the 'Ladies'.
I fidgeted my impatience.
"Sit still, ‘Intestinal worm of a cat’!", commanded he, who has such a way with words. I instantly obeyed and he continued...
"And so it is with women."

Ah! It was out! The word 'Women'! Oh, wonderful, juicy and delectable word.
Women, women, women!
"Now; 'Winkle-Brain', I shall continue on my journey into the Druidic mysteries of womanhood. You know, of course that the Druids, of ancient times, worshipped trees purely as some form of sexual interpretation... Wood, you see... Trees and magic berries.".
'He who walks the heavens' leaned forward in a conspiratorial fashion and I gained full sense of his aura.
Druids? Trees? I made up my mind to remember those words and look them up as soon as I could.
"Thus, 'Speck on an incontinent pad', we come to a conclusion that those females who come from colder climes are pliable, supple and more likely to bend to a man's will, once a man know where the heart lies. In a nutshell...Those ladies who act cold and careless are the very ones who burn the easiest once you have fired them up. You might perceive them as ice-like but once the bark is stripped."
Here, 'He, who walks the heavens' lifted his eyes upwards.
"My God! Do they have a burning passion so bright, that you can fashion anything from their pliability!"
So saying, my sainted elder sibling stood up in magnificence, eyes alive with his own thoughts of savage conquests while I, in all innocence, stared up

at his figure in awe...He was my 'Lord'! He was my very 'King!'

"But your hardwood woman is made of sterner stuff, far more resilient and lasting for an eternity."

'He who walks the heavens' had now re-seated himself, his voice soft in reverie.

"Ah, 'Hardwood women', matriarchal to the core. You understand?", he asked.

I didn't but my wise head nodded.

"Think on it.", he said, ignoring my nodding head.

"You go to your hot countries, Italy, Israel, Malta. Wherever; you will find that the female is always in charge. Matriarchal society, you see?".

My nods livened although I was now completely lost. Was there a moral to this story? I mean, I didn't know what a moral was, but I liked things simple, 'Mother-Goose' simple.

"And the moral here is...".

'Oh lordy, lordy!'. The font of all wisdom could actually read my mind! I steadied my brain to reason as this sainted man continued…

"If you choose a cold sort of woman, you know for sure you can get away with murder once you melt the heart. But the fiery women, the hardwoods, the tough-nuts; you need a sharp tool to keep them in trim and can always guarantee that they come from a matriarchal family.".

I was still sitting, floor-bound, as my brother left the room, smiling slightly as he glanced back at my puzzled expression.

So what was it all about? Even now I have no idea but one thing I do know is that my mother runs this household, as her mother does hers...And both have a fiery nature with 'Furnace-Hot' red hair!
I deduced from the lecture that women from cold countries were more easily manipulated than those from hot countries, and that those from hot countries had an inbred desire to run the household and family within it.
But what puzzled me, the question which remained was, how does one tell what country a woman comes from? The only give-away would be if the lady in question had red hair, other than that, one had to literally interrogate the lady, to find out the answer.

CHAPTER FOUR.

‘THE RAGING HORMONES.’

It was not the happiest times for me, in that it seemed even the ugliest of women drew my eyes to their figures. I seemed to find hidden joys in every part of them, the clear beauty of their eyes, the small tremble of their lower lips as they spoke, the smell of their nearness, the secret form their clothes hid… Oh, indeed, I am a most un-happiest of people, I tell you. Even yesterday, I found myself staring at my mother's very best friend, Martha Evergreen-Stokes, with avid eyes! That, dear readers, is how desperately sad I am and how I need to understand more about this condition I am in. I need more knowledge about the 'Secrets of Women'!

And so, understanding my sainted elder sibling's need to rest from my 'Over inquisitive' nature, I settled for second best and now sat before Spotty Watson's father.

A problem here was that 'The Teller of Tall Tales' was disinclined to talk about women. It would seem that, having received a summons from the local Job-Centre, to attend a meeting in the very short future, to discuss finding him a job, Spotty Watson's father was more inclined to talk about finance and the means of gaining it.

Spotty had been dispatched, to locate and buy a medical book which would give the symptoms of Sciatica. This, Spotty Watson's father assured us, was a most ingenious way of confusing the medical profession, that problems of the back and nervous systems and the pains thereof, were very hard to fathom and medical certificates were handed out to all and sundry, rather than send the patient for a costly and time-consuming hospital examination.

And so, I sat alone, in front of the 'Teller of Tall Tales' as he acquainted me with the facts of finance.

I will tell you, dear readers, it is quite hard to keep an interested visage on display, when the mind worries over other factors which unsettle the life. However; I really am very good at concealment, this coming from my sneaky and foxy nature, so I listened with a seemingly composed interest as Spotty Watson's father spoke.

"When it comes to money… Always be poor.", he began.

Now, to me, most men would sooner die than admit poverty. Why, even the poorest beggar has a tin mug in which the rich would sacrifice a few pennies, the beggar might then count his wealth at the end of the day. This thought, I brought to his attention.

"But, my boy.", he replied. "If people know you have money, they will ask to borrow some... This leaves you with the problem of having to think up excuses as to why you cannot lend."

Spotty Watson's father allowed me the time to digest this information by lifting a bare foot up across his knee and digging at his toenails with the sharp point of a safety-pin. It is hard to keep any concentrated thought while the eyes are in line with such an action. Focusing my mind and by lowering my eyes, I considered the facts of what this wise man had said. Yes, it made sense to my young, uninformed, mind and I said as much, that, in this case, it would be very astute to deny any sense of wealth. Nodding with wise confidence, Spotty Watson's father shifted positions, now examining the other foot, before saying… "But money is important and the more one can borrow, the more the power.".

Oh yes, I might have been young and uncertain about life but I surely knew that money gave you power, the power to buy all the sweets, the comics, the presents which encourage a girl to allow a kiss… Oh, my mind was confused with the thoughts of such spending power...

"I will tell you something.", he said in conspiratorial tone, breaking into my thoughts... "If you have one coin to your name, then get it changed into smaller coinage. Failing that, beg another from someone, someone will always give you a small coin or two, it makes them feel smugly superior in the giving.".

I was given time to consider this fact, giving consideration to this mental genius as he put the foot down and, grimacing, with all teeth showing, shifted his body sideways to allow the mornings food-content to escape in a most satisfying sound. My smile and shine of eyes greeted the ‘Whoosh’ with applause. Re-settling, with a grand outburst of sighed relief, he continued…

“Once you have more than one coin in your pocket, you shake them, make them rattle.".

"Why?"

Spotty Watson’s father smiled as my thin voiced pierced the air.

"Because, young man; if you rattle the change, people will think you have money. And you will notice that institutions like banks and societies are always willing to lend others who have money. It's a sense of collateral you see; if they think you have money, and the jingle from your pocket assures then you have, they will always be willing to lend you more.".

Wasn’t he wonderfully knowledgeable? This ‘Teller of Tall Tales’ was truly a fount of all wisdom!

“Indeed, my boy; in life, always be poor!”, he concluded, before settling back to his foot-digging.

Spotty had returned from his errand, having secured from the library, a copy of a fine red-bound medical book.

Spotty and I left his father's presence, he engrossed in his reading. Spotty led me to the street-door, before stopping to select a number of walking-sticks from an umbrella stand, as his father had directed.

Thus; I left, still concerned about my future and the amorous sensations which fostered themselves on my impatient soul.

Such was the time, until…

There are times in ones life when the power of divinity does surely wane. The matter of this fact was that my brother, 'He, who walks the heavens', was spending more and more time with the 'Siren' who dwells in my mind's heaven, the Lady Maureen Soap.

I, too, in a new sense of maturity, had become more adult and found love within my class at school. For there, in her ravishing newness, sat the beautiful Alison!

Oh, had I not closed up my eyes in adoration and hope, that this delightful creature would see in me the Adonis, the power of all love which I directed her way. It is true, I had not spoken to her, for, if I did, I was sure the spell of this powerful love would be broken. And I know from my readings of Shakespeare, that love is a silent art, a whispered awe of silence. Thus, was I silent in my passion, while my mind, in forgetful pose, sought less inspiration from my sainted elder sibling.

Strange then, as my mind and heart pulsed with such a love that I hardly felt the smart tap to my skull.

“Steady as she blows, ‘Young insignificant’.”.

“I am sorry my Lord.”, I said, instinctively adopting the pose of a vassal before his master, the whispered lisp an offering, as I rubbed at the, now, smartening hurt.

“Sorry, indeed. You seem to wander these halls without the slightest idea of direction. What ails you, ‘Smallest of entrails?”.

“ I must confess to you, my Lord, that my mind is quite full these days.”

If I had stopped to rationalise, I would have realised that I had spoken up in quite a manly way to this all-powerful of men. I had straightened my frame, my voice almost as an equal.

“Ah, ‘Young frailty’, you are in love!”, exclaimed this giant, smiling with golden eyes at my awe-filled surprise.

“Why? What makes you say that, Sir?”, I stammered.

“Ah ha! You are of that age! Raging Hormones!”

Oh, my Sainted Lord, did my mind whirl!

‘Raging Hormones’!

These words were the very sense of my mindless confusion. My adoration for the lovely Alison was a derangement,which the wise refer to as the ‘Raging Hormones’!

So am I well informed by ‘He who walks the heavens’, The ‘Grand Master’ of wisdom.

“I am unwell, my Lord.”, I gasped, clutching at the doorpost, holding myself in an upright position. In a strange way, I felt a dark hole of despair and ill-feeling engulf me.

“Do I die, my Lord?”

“No; unless you refuse to do exactly as I say, young simpleton. The choice is yours. Should you take your own road, then you will see and feel, in the beginning, small ulcerated spots which will quickly spread.”

“I will do all you ask, my Lord.”, I quickly pledged.

‘He who walks the heavens’ paused, inspecting my face, as if already seeing the start of the ‘Raging Hormones’.

“At present, ‘Smallest of turds’, your face seems quite intact. I believe we have caught it just in time.”

These words exposed to me a glimmer of hope, that this giant, this angelic Lord would, once again, be my saving grace, my mighty protector.

“Follow, young ‘Spermatic Simpleton’.”, instructed my sainted elder sibling. “I will endeavor to explain the complications and mysticisms of your torment.”.

Now, gentle readers; only the most uncommon of fools would not follow this intrepid explorer of knowledge, for he was a David Livingstone of knowledge. A man who opened up the darkest trails of deepest Africa. I would follow ‘He, who walks the heavens’ into any obscurity, so that I, in my stupidity and ignorance, discover the awesome truth of ‘Ranging Hormones’.

Seating himself in his favorite chair, enthroned, as it appeared to me, ‘He, who walks the heavens’, first demanded that I, ‘Pimple-Winkle’, provide him with a cup of tea plus the last of the high-tea cream cakes, a truly holy nourishment, which I had fully intended to rescue later and indulge my greed.

Thus; did I go, a ready servant, to the kitchen and set myself to the task. I found it somewhat hard to fulfill my duty in astute manner simply because it is quite hard to move easily when ones eyes are squeezed tight shut for a good deal of the time. It had not struck me, until reaching the ‘Room of Chores’, that there were hung, at intervals, sections of polished mirror. I had been informed, earlier, by the ‘He who walks the heavens, these mirrors were placed there so that our father, whilst at his household duties, might view himself and realise the disenchantment of Holy Matrimony.

Still… I digress…

It was, on seeing the high reflection of the mirrors, I feared that I might catch sight of the beginnings of the ravages of the dread 'Raging Hormones', the pits and ulcerated caverns which would scar my face. Thus, with eyes closed, except for brief 'Quick-Sight' flashes which illuminated memory, I evaded the sight of my countenance, should the ulceration have started. Carefully, I padded my form back to where 'He who walks the heavens' sat. I waited for the nod of acquiescence which complied with a job well done. The nod came, and with it I sat at the feet of my 'Lord', as he began to explain the horrors of 'Raging Hormones'.

"Raging Hormones", he began. "Is a plague which is descended upon the weakness of young boys, such as yourself."

"Please Sir.", I interjected, a question wrinkling the tip of my nose and agitating my small frame so that I squirmed like a worm on a hook.

"Well, ,Tear of a sweat-gland'. What is it?"

He, who is Holiness exalted, glanced down at me in an irritated lifting of eyebrows.

"Please, my Lord, do girls get the 'Raging Hormones' as well?"

Oh, by my own heart, I dared not to breath as my 'Lord' twisted his mouth into a thought-mode. My mind savaged itself in unfathomable fear. If girls did get such a disease, I would surely die of a broken heart. I knew, from a secret searching (Which cost me some of my best marbles, for Spotty Watson to get the answer from teachers register.) I knew my sweet Alison, she who outshone even 'Helen of Troy', was but one month older than I. So, I realised, if girls got this dread disease as did boys, then she, too, would bear the ravages of 'Raging Hormones'!

Oh, my sweet, sweet, loved brother, tell me it is not so! So raged my mind as wide anxious eyes peered up at my Lord, the height of all beings.

"No, young 'Septic-Tank'. Girls do not get 'Raging Hormones.".

There…! It was out!…And my breath whooshed out from me as does the air from a balloon when it is held in such a way that the noise blurbs out like a longest of farts.

"And I shall tell you why!"

This sudden statement from my 'Lord' brought my exertions to a stop, my exhilaration, at not imagining my sweet-love's face gradually scramble into a mess of ‘Pizza-Like’ zits, even worse than Spotty Watson’s!

“Girls.”, continued ‘He, who walks the heavens’, “Flower in a most secret way.”

Flower! Secret!

Oh the joy of these words to my poetic mind. To consider; my sweet Alison would ‘Flower’, in a secret way’!

“Will I ever learn the secret, my Lord?”

‘He, who walks the heavens’, eyed me in a rather disdainful way, before saying, “ No man knows of such secrets…But…”

And here, my sainted brother held such a long breath of intelligence that I nearly burst in the certain knowledge that ‘He, who is the eighth wonder of all worlds’, surely knew things which no other mortal might know. His breath was released in a wealth of acknowledgement, of import.

“Young pip of an ulcerated camels’ dung; I will tell you on one understanding…That not a word of what I say leaves these halls of residence.”.

Well, my head nodded so much acquiescence that my teeth rattled in the excitement.

“Please tell, my Lord... Please do!”

I squirmed as if my bowels might burst, aware that my earnest assurances would gain me information that even Spotty Watson's father did not know! I would be 'King' among men in my classroom with this power of knowledge.

"A Red Rose".

He, who delights all angels, had leaned back, his leonine head seeking a higher ceiling as he pushed the words towards my eager ears.

"A Red Rose…"

I echoed his words with whispered devotion, my eyes drawn upwards, seeking the same angels which, I am sure, my sainted brother saw, aware, too, that the small hairs on the back of my neck were now raised in agitated fear.

"A Red Rose.", I whispered again, understanding now the full import of the oath I had sworn, never to divulge this secret information.

If I kept this information a secret, then surely the ravages of 'Raging Hormones' would become less spiteful. I entwined my fingers into a 'Crossed Lace' as we do in our 'Gang', when making the sworn oath of 'Eternal secrecy, on pain of death', swearing on this oath to keep this secret of the 'Red Rose'.

"What is the Red Rose, my Lord?"

In my awe, I had not really discovered exactly what the 'Red Rose' was! Oh, I was aware that it was of some truly great significance, else 'He who walks the heavens' would never have imparted such information.

"Ah, 'Bubble of sperm'.", said my sainted brother, a whisk of smile deepening the cherry of his lips, his eyes drifting down from the heights to face my earnestness.

"I will tell you."

Here, my brother rubbed a gently sculptured hand across his chin, eying me in dubious fashion, as if now undecided whether to trust me with such a secret. My eyes, dimmed in tear's fashion, begged him to enlighten me, till, as if deciding, he nodded in confirmation.

"Yes, I will tell you…Now, bend an ear."

My ears were the size of Dumbo's at this command, elephantine appendages which literally drooped to the floor.

"I am all ears, my Lord."

Here, 'He who walks the heavens' began to acquaint me with the secret of the 'Red Rose'.

"At a certain time in a young girls' life, she becomes affected by a great sadness. It is called 'Depression'.

There is nothing can be done for the young lady, she is left to ride this emotional storm until the girl's mother goes to see Old Woman Rozzerman.".

"Old Woman Rozzerman?"

I did not mean to speak out and very grateful that my sainted elder sibling seemed not too perturbed that I had, for he smiled as he watched the puzzle chase its expression across my face. I might explain that Old Woman Rozzerman owned the general grocery store at the end of our street. It is true, I had seen many women going in and out of this store, but I assumed this was for groceries.

My mind whirled at all this imparted information. I still have yet to find out what 'Red Rose' was. And 'Depression'? From my studies at school I knew that depressions were hollowed out holes of sorts.

Now, this was a puzzle; we have a secret 'Red Rose' and an old shop-keeper and a depressed hole… It did not make sense!

Then, 'He who walks the heavens' decided to enlighten me further.

"Consider this, 'Leavings of the Scarab'. You might well think that Old Woman Rozzerman is just an old lady who runs a general store. Well, now I will tell you a real secret. Up and down this country, even in every country of the world, there are corner-shops which are run by old women, like Old Woman

Rozzerman. These elderly women are not the normal run of beings. They deal in witchcraft!"

"Witchcraft!", he exclaimed again, louder and with demonic intensity. 'He, who walks the heavens', had eyes as wide as saucers, that I feared they would pop out and roll off down the hallway. Such was my fear at these words, I was hard pushed to stifle a scream, gagging my mouth with a fist. I realised, of course, that I should not fear while 'My Lord' watched over me. His noble face had resumed equal proportions and I quieted my terrified mind. I know that this abode of ours held evil secrets and forms of devil-worship. Indeed; I had once overheard my father tell his brother, my Uncle Joseph, that my beloved mother was a witch…And more, that her mother was the spawn of evil! And it was then I had realised that within my fathers' fragile frame was great courage, for he had laughed loudly as he spoke those words, laughter in the face of such gravity. But, then again; my father would have had to have such a courage, as to pass such genes through to my 'Lord', my sainted brother . Perhaps it was true of my small frame, that the juice of my making had been strained through a handkerchief as 'He, who walks the heavens' had once informed me, so that I lacked the strength and mind to walk among the clouds.

"They are all witches?

My mind had returned to normality, causing me to clarify this situation, that all women who managed corner-shop stores were witches.

"Think on, my young unsubstantial sibling… It is a fact that you are in love, are you not?"

Oh, my sweet brother… Do you not feel this thumping heart, this swelling within me when my mind conjures up the fair face of beloved Alison! Such were the words I wanted to scream out. Instead, I simply nodded a weak gesture, as though ashamed of such feelings…And even my nod of agreement was half-hearted, in that, had it not been for the fact that 'He, who knows all things' could read my mind, I would have denied all knowledge of this sweet love for Alison. I blushed in confusion and kept eyes downcast.

"Do you not see now, 'Pimple-Winkle', how even a young girl can twist your mind till you can think of nothing else?"

I acknowledged the fact, raising my eyes in the understanding that even he, who is the adoration of all females, knew of such a powerful feeling.

"And so.", said he, in conclusion… "All women have this magic power over we males."

"Except you, my Lord."

‘He, who walks the heavens ‘, smiled in no small amusement. Oh, did my heart fly when this wonderful of all men smiled in honest affection. Pride rose as tears welled in my eyes.

“Even I, my young simpleton, can be caught if I gaze too fondly into the eyes of any Medusa, who reaches to rob me of my ‘Snake’, to add to the locks she already has.”.

Medusa?… Snakes?…Such talk was beyond me, although it had to be that my dear elder sibling, is obviously a master in the ‘Dungeons and Dragons’ of life, that he has the power and strength to deny any ‘Magic Lady or Witch’, who tried to charm his ‘Snake’ from him, whatever this ‘Snake’ was!

“But the elderly crones, such as Old Woman Rozzerman, hold the secrets of magic and are able to prepare a concoction which will bring all young ladies out of their ‘Depression’.”

Such words as my glorious brother spoke, awoke my mind to the lesson in hand. While my sainted brother scratched at his nose with a delicate finger, I had time to collect my thoughts, placing them in order.

So; at a time in a young girls life, a ‘Depression’, a hole opens up. This ‘Depression’ then causes the mother of the girl to visit the crone, Old Woman Rozzerman, who runs the corner-shop. Now; this elderly witch makes up a parcel of some magic brew which, one supposes, the mother takes home to give the daughter.

“And this magic cure the mother gives to her daughter cures her?”, I asked, having reached my conclusion and bringing the attention of ‘My Lord’ back to our conversation.

“Huh?”, he said.

I was quiet for a while, ashamed at my intrusion, for I am sure the ‘He, who walks the heavens’ was with the Angels, conversing with those ‘Haloed Beings’, this fact becoming more obvious as he dropped beautiful blue eyes to my questioning face, the higher ‘Light of Heaven’ drifting from his beautiful visage, a return to normality.

“Oh, yes.”, he said, after a while, now more compliant… “ I will tell you of this magic cure.”.

I dare not move in case I missed even one syllable of this secret ‘Telling’.

“ In all cases of a young girls ’Depression’, the mother is given a parcel to take home, with instructions that the mother should wait until her daughter lies in a stupor, a sleep induced by powders of ‘Asprin’ which take away certain cramp-like pains.”.

Here; my mind whirled in sympathetic pain, that my sweet Alison would suffer such ‘Cramp-Like’ pains.

Oh, Sweet Lord! Would it be that I, 'Pimple-Winkle' could have that pain transferred to my body. Would I scream in agony, yet know in my mind that my sweet love is saved from such savage torture. Thus would I surely die for my love!

"Now!", snapped 'My Lord', in a certain agitation, realising that my mind was in wander. I sat up, rationalising my mind for any import this 'Majestic Person' might impart. Satisfied at my attention, he continued...

"Once the mother is assured her daughter lies in slumber, she unwraps the parcel. From this parcel comes a 'Red Rose', in full bloom, still fresh with dew, as if plucked from the sainted earth that very moment. Gently, with a small devout prayer on her lips, the mother places the 'Red Rose' between the thighs of her daughter, so that, on waking, the young girl discovers just the damp dew of the 'Red Rose', because the magic flower has become the scented 'Water of Womanhood'."

Oh, my giddy saints!

This magic, this secret tale given to me by 'He, who walks the heavens', has opened up a picture of such magnificence, that I sat in my amazement, allowing such a divine significance to be framed in golden form. I thrilled to this knowledge of the 'Red Rose', understanding that young girls grew from soft and gentle buds to 'Full-bloomed Roses'!

Oh, my giddy mind!

I promise on the 'Blood of the Red Rose' that none of my new found knowledge would ever be passed on to any other, even to Spotty Watkins, not for all my marbles back, not even for the giant 'Black Whirl' marble he kept next to his heart in a small leather bag!

It then struck me, not that I was glad for my sweet-love Alison, that she would be saved from the ravages of the 'Raging Hormones'. But what of me, how would I fare?

"How would I fare?" I asked, somewhat abruptly, my train of mind allowing me to search the answer in a loud voice.

'He, who walks the heavens', rose from his chair, as if in annoyance, that I, 'Pimple-Winkle', had dared raise my voice to high uncomfortable volume.

"You will have to wait, 'Essence of Armpit', till I return from my slumbers.".

Before leaving me with my thoughts, he turned… "And I will tell you about the 'Juices of Testosterone' which all young boys have to face, which is a saving grace, saving you from facial disfigurations and allowing the growth of 'The Snake Which Wriggles'!.

Oh, did I fear these words, which were uttered in a hissed whisper, as if from the mouth of a very 'Snake' itself!…I listened, hearing my sainted elder sibling laugh in devilish glee, listening till the sound diminished, leaving the echo which played its fearsome music to my mind.

"Mornings", had said Spotty Watson's father. "Are the companions of expectations. It don't matter whether they are good or bad, it's another day and we meet it with expectation.".

I write this now, simply because I had not seen 'He who walks the heavens' since he had retired to his bedroom. I had spent a rather sleepless night and now it was the creeping light of a morning. Lying there, I did truly have with me the company of expectation. For some reason, I had expected to find my face completely eroded. Yet, on a hand-feeling expedition, I felt the smooth and supple skin of a youth. You would have to understand that this experiment was carried out with my eyes closed. As every boy knows, the 'Waking' is never a wide-eyed experience, a sudden opening of the eyes. The 'Waking' is a slow and gradual opening, whereby the eyes first flicker, then become mere slits of blurred awareness until the adjustment to light is allowed, in a slow unhurried lift, until the eyes are wide in wakefulness.

In this way did I wake, gradually.

Then in sudden alarm, as my vision centered itself on the thing before my eyes.

A red blur!

I blinked hard, not once but numerous times and each time, the red blur beamed bright like a warning light. My hands, now shaking in fear, reached up and traced my visage, moving in and now, with a horrid knowledge, realized that, on my earlier investigation, my fingers had not touched my nose. Now, my fingers gently zoned in on this facial object, moving so that I could see and feel that the red blur was on the tip of my nose and, by a more cross-eyed inspection, I could see it in its more raised definition. It was a 'Zit'… The largest red spot in the world!

This was it! This was the beginning of the 'Raging Hormones', the start of complete ulceration! I was finished as a mere mortal, my bones in cleansed whiteness as the flesh was gradually eaten away by this creeping 'Zit-Monster'.

Crawling from the bed, I felt the weakness in my legs, holding onto the bedside cabinet and making my way to the door in a slow and torturous stoop. I could feel the flesh of my nose begin to burn, the will to survive being tested to its utmost.

In a gigantic effort, I made it to the door of my elder and most sainted sibling, knowing in my heart that only he could save me. In this weakened state, holding onto the door-jamb. I managed to tap on the door.

“Help me, my Lord.”

“What do you want, ‘Septic-Tank?”

‘He, who walks the heavens’, had thrown open the door and stood in all magnificence, the scarlet smoking jacket aloud to his frame.

“I am dying, my Lord.”

“ Good gracious, you have a ‘Cherry’!”

“A ‘Cherry’, my lord?”

“Yes. A ‘Cherry’. Right there, on the end of your nose.”

The word, ‘Cherry’ seemed to ring a bell, a distant clanging in the recess of my mind, but in my present state I dismissed the ringing.

“Am I to die then, my Lord… How long do I have before the ‘Raging Hormones’ wipes my face from the ends of the earth?”

“Good grief, ‘Young nose-drippings’, you wont die from this. It might give total facial disfigurement, but you wont die.”

I breathed a sigh of relief at this most welcome news. The fact that I would have to wear something akin to a paper bag over my head did not worry me as much as the fact that the 'Raging Hormones' might kill me.

"I will tell you something, young simpleton, you might try a dab of perfume on the 'Cherry'. It will stop the pus from running and dry the scab."

There, once again, this proves that 'He who walks the heavens' had such a wonderful knowledge.

"Might I borrow some from you, my Lord?", I asked.

"Men do not use perfume, 'Spermatic squirt'. Go and ask mother for some."

With that, my sainted elder sibling closed the door, almost catching my nose and flattening the 'Cherry' all over my face.

I was alone in my agony. Then, in spite of my pain, I crept to the top of the stairs, hearing distant voices rising as my parents talked. Silently, I crept to my mother's bedroom and entered. The bottles and liquid assortments stared back at me from the dressing table.

"Parfume La Vie.".

I read the label and, removing the stopper, sniffed at its contents, jerking back as the scent stabbed at my nostrils, seeming to send a strong message of acid to my brain. However; since 'He who walks the heavens' had stated that this would cease the spread of the 'Cherry' in some way, I would comply with his direction. Taking a wad of cotton wool from a container, I poured some of the perfume on and plastered it to my nose.

The sudden stinging and pain brought tears to my eyes, my mouth opening to utter such a fearsome scream of pain, that I quickly grabbed hold of the bed-sheet, the end of which I jammed into my mouth. It was some time before I could breath in a correct manner, though it took a lot longer before the spasmodic jerking of my body ceased.

Returning to my bedroom, I knew I would have to find a cure for this decease, before the ravages tore the very flash from my bones. I would have to get my sainted elder sibling to tell me the secret before it was too late.

Meanwhile; I had to find a way to rid myself of the evil smell which seemed to invade the bedroom as soon as I entered.

'Parfume La Vie.', really was a powerful source of determination, seduction in a most fluid form. It also made me realize why my father had a most flawless skin! … This I add as an after-thought.

CHAPTER FIVE.

‘THE TELLING OF THE SECRET.’

The next two days held their own. By that, I mean, the perfume seemed to have done the trick, in as far as keeping the 'Raging Hormones' at bay. The 'Cherry' had now toned itself down to a small circle of reddening, as if someone had pinched the end of my nose hard. Spotty Watson's father had made a smallest of remarks about my nose, considering it to be somewhat enhancing, saying…

"Anything unusual is an attraction as it draws the eyes. Think of a man with a large nose, like Punch. Everyone loves Punch. And, do you know…"

Here, Spotty Watson's father eased himself into speech as does a rather fat lady 'Ease' herself into a chair…

"Oliver Cromwell was most attractive to the ladies of his day, even though his face was riddled with walts. And Cyrano De Bergerac ha a most enormous nose, but loved by all the ladies. Then there was the Roman Emperor, Julius Caesar… He had…"

" A nose 'Roaming' all over his face…"

My voice trailed away as Spotty Watson's father glared at me, before trumpeting a most loud fart.

"What I mean is…", continued this most talented man. "Any disfigurement can be most appealing to a ladies eye."

" Look at the Hunchback of Notre Dame and Esmeralda!", exclaimed Spotty Watson.

I must state that I fully expected Spotty's father to subject Spotty to a similar glare as I had received. Instead, Spotty received a most beneficial smile of allowance , I suspected some sense of favoritism going on. I let the feeling pass, after all, was not Spotty Watson the son of this 'Teller of Tall Tales', and deserving of any favour. Mind you, Spotty seemed to have all the graces of those above, in that, with his 'Pizza-Face', he was sure to appeal to all the ladies in the land. How lucky was my very best friend, Spotty Watson!

What Spotty Watson's father had to say about facial disfigurement was quite appeasing and I worried less about the ravages of the 'Raging Hormones'.

Until the next morning.

There is a 'Law', some form of 'Home-Spun' philosophy, which states that things happen when you least expect them, the 'Glitch', as Spotty Watson's father had called it.
My 'Glitch' was one of shock and dismay, yet followed by a marvelous piece of luck. Might I liken it to losing a pound note and finding a penny. But, finding the penny coin was one of a rare date and worth thousands of pounds!

The morning after my meeting with Spotty Watson's father, and his speech which lessened my worries, I awoke in fine fettle. So much so that I sprang out of bed with the joyous knowledge it was Monday morning and soon I would be in school, there to gaze with love on the very beautiful Alison. With a song in my heart and her sweet face in my mind's eye, I ran to bathroom, intending to spruce myself up to a high degree.

Then… Oh. my Good Lord in Heavens above!

There, in reflection from the mirror, I saw that a new spot had 'Pussed' itself to my face, just to the right of my nose. Unlike the now softened red glow of the 'Lamp-Zit' at the end of my nose, this new outbreak was a purplish outer ring with a yellowing head. I knew that this new attack was like a mole, burrowing its poison deep into the flesh, boring into the soft bone beneath. The sight of its head made me realize the truth of the saying that 'Mountains are made out of molehills', that fear does enlarge the scope.

You might remember, gentle readers, that I earlier stated that the dismay I suffered at finding the new' Zit-Attack', was followed by a turn of events which, at least, paid me some back-dividends. It came about as I was staggering back to my bedroom, when…
" Ah, 'Pimple-Winkle'… Just the very brat I need!"
'He, who walks the heavens' had stepped out of his bedroom and held up a restraining hand.
"I am unwell, my Lord.", I whispered, hoping that my most unwell voice would inspire some sympathy.
"Of course you are unwell, 'Septic-Tank'. An insipid stripling with such a build and brain as yours would

bound to be unwell."
Of course, all that my most sainted elder sibling said was perfectly true. How dare I expect any smallest amount of sympathy from such a valiant warrior as he. I raised tear-filled eyes to his magnificent face, my eyebrows raised.
"You have need of me, my Lord?"
"Yes, 'Small Insignificance'… Indeed I do need your voice. Today, I am to visit a friend, which means I shall not be in or available to any who wish to see me."
I nodded my understanding, though unsure why my sainted elder sibling should apprise me of the fact that he would be unavailable.
"Now, 'Toad-Skin'… I want you, around midday, to go to Maureen's house and tell her I am unwell and that I will not be able to see her tonight."
Thus, was I now apprised of wat this sainted man needed me for. I would be his errand-boy.
I have mentioned to you, in earlier times, that my mind can work in an exceedingly devious way. And such was the way my mind, it caused me to immediately react, so my pose adopted a most sinister effect, my eyes downcast as my hands 'Dry-Washed' themselves.
"Are you ill, my Lord?"
My voice had taken on the soft lisping of one who humbles themself, yet, at the same time, realizes one has the upper hand.
"Of course I am well, you young 'Patter of

Urination'!"
'He who walks the heavens' had an impatience in his voice which is, normally, the very warning before a sharp tug of the ear is felt. But I continued in my insistence…
"Then you ask me to tell an untruth, my Lord. That I should tell a falsehood to the Lady Maureen Soap?"
My hands fumbled over each other, my voice more prominent in its lisp.
"What are you on about…Oh, I see… It's blackmail again."
I kept my eyes down as I heard his voice, at first, in thunderous tone, then trail off into the softness of realization.
"I am your most obedient servant, my Lord… I am the slime which clings to the sole of your shoe…I am…"
"Stop talking rubbish, 'Pimple-Winkle' and tell me what you want?"
"I would like you to tell me how I am to rid myself of the 'Raging Hormones, my Lord, before I am eaten alive."
Turning away, 'He who walks the heavens' made his way back into his bedroom, then, turning again, he drew me with his finger… "Come in here", he ordered, holding open the door to his bedroom.
Oh, my Giddy Aunt! I am frozen in this glorified sense of delight and feel quite light-headed, as if some electrifying heavenly light was now beamed down on me! To be asked into the highest of

sanctums, the Shangri La, the Elysian Field…
"Come, Pimple-Winkle!".
This urgent demand, made by 'He, who walks the heavens' awoke me to the reality of my standing, that I, smallest of a 'Dung Beetles' entrails, am summoned to my Lords boudoir.

I entered…

I am in another world, entranced. From a darkened ceiling, there twinkled a scrabble of lights, small stars which seemed to roam the night sky. My nostrils were open to the scent of perfumed candles, which added an aura of opulence to the room. My feet sunk into a deep pile of white carpet, which brought my gaze to the black silk sheets. I stood, my mouth aghast at the sheer magic of this room, this bedroom drama. 'He, who walks the heavens' had smiled at my gawking, then, in a magnificent gesture, spread his joyful frame out onto the large bed, a very Anthony, waiting for his Cleopatra to arrive.
"Seat yourself, 'Fragrance of Feet', and tell me what it is you would like to know?"
I sat, as indicated, on a small footstool by the bed, my eyes still wandering around the room, still discovering new treasures, the mirrors and pictures which adorned the walls.
"Well, insect?"
"I wish you to tell me how I might protect myself

from the ravages of the 'Raging Hormones', my Lord.", I said, dragging my eyes away from the gold-framed pictures of semi-naked goddesses.

'He, who walks the heavens' raised himself onto one elbow.

"And… If I tell you? What services are you prepared to render to me?"

"I shall do your bidding until eternity, my Lord. I will spread rose petals at your feet as you walk. I shall extol your virtues to the world. I will…"

"Smallest of a knat's droppings… I do not wish you to go that far… I mean, about the rose petals. But if you promise to do my bidding, to polish my shoes each day, to carry my messages to whom I tell you, without question"

"Oh, my Lord, indeed I shall! Your every wish is my command. I will work for you till my eyelids droop from tiredness, till these frail hands no longer work. I will…"

"Enough!"

I stopped in my offerings as 'He, who walks the heavens' held up a hand and then sat on the edge of the bed.

"When I was about your age, 'Changeling', I had to suffer the same experience as you do now."

I stared at this sainted man in disbelief, for I could never envisage this 'Divinity' as ever being 'My Age'. Nor, in a million years, could I make my mind conjure up any 'Zit; daring to mar such a perfect skin.

"When I was about your age…" again my sainted elder sibling repeated, seeing my eyes cloud in their wandering and, seeing alertness descend to them once more, continued, "I set off to seek the advice of a Guru, who lived in a small village in the hills of Katmandu. The journey, through dangerous jungles, which had me avoiding deadly tribes of savages, at last had me arrive at the hut of a very wise man."
I sat, entranced, my imagination following this intrepid adventure, risking the perils, seeing this magnificent man, as a boy, fighting his way through the deadly jungles.
'He, who walks the heavens' lay back on the bed, sinking into the dark silk of the sheets, his eyes tracing the stars which twinkled from the ceiling.
"This Guru.", he continued. "Had skin which had seen a thousand years and eyes of a milky white luminescence, that would change colour as moods reflected his feelings. He wore just a few old rags, shapeless. But his voice seemed to come from all around, from the earth and sky. I seated myself before this Guru, not fearful, but proud and upright."

My mind had been with this proud boy, shading his journey and witnessing his seating before the Guru. I sat more upright, in respect for the courage which my sainted elder sibling had shown throughout the ordeal. I am afraid my courage would have failed me, even before the start of the journey. Oh, 'Joy of heavens', that I have such a wonderful elder sibling

as this, who spares me such an ordeal.
"There is no need to speak, said the Guru, before I could open my mouth.", continued 'He, who walks the heavens', "For I know why you come. At this, I remained silent. The Guru had me sit for some time, then began to tell me what I needed to hear."
I leaned forward.
"What did he tell you, my Lord?"
"The Guru said in a soft voice… I know you, boy. I know a million like you. You are as many as the leaves on the trees, you sigh for knowledge, for the 'Secrets'. You are here to learn the secret of the 'De-flowering', that which will save you from the ravages of the 'Raging Hormones'."

My heart raced in an experience of excitement, as does one who having reached the 'Tomb of the 'Lost Pharaoh of Egypt', is about to open the door, to expose the lost treasures. My eyes urged my sainted elder sibling to continue.

"I will explain to you.", continued my brother. "What is to be done, what you must do which will turn you from a stripling into a 'Man of beauty'."

I listened to 'He, who walks the heavens' as if in some strange kind of fantasy, in some entranced dream, hearing his voice, yet unaware that his lips moved as he spoke. The room seemed to glow as the candles burned their incense, their light casting weird shadows on the walls. I shook my head into some sense of cohesion as ‘He, who walks the heavens’ spoke on.

“There are two things you have to do, instructed the Guru, before you can rid yourself of the ‘Raging Hormones’. First you must mix yourself a drink, a fierce brew which is known as the ‘Juices of Testosterone’. This ancient potion is only known to a few of us, and because of your determination and bravery, I am now going to tell you. The ‘Juices of Testosterone’ has to be made up under the light of a ‘Midnight Moon’, seated beneath an old oak tree. The ‘Juice’ consists of two clothes of Garlic, crushed into a drop of olive oil and one red Chili, also crushed. I will warn you, this potion is not to be drunk until a certain time, the time of the ‘De-Flowering’”.

My mind was busy, storing this information, so busy that when I opened my eyes to gaze at my sainted elder sibling, it appeared that he had drifted off into some sort of trance. I waited, afraid that I would not hear the rest of the ‘Telling’. I understood there were two parts to the dismissal of the ‘Raging Hormones’. I had the first part, about the potion… But what about the time of the ‘De-Flowering’?

“What about the ‘De-Flowering’, my Lord?”, I heard myself ask.

He who walks the heavens opened his eyes wide, having borrowed the light of angels so his eyes shone a most heavenly blue. He smiled.

"This is what the aged Guru told me.", he said. "I was told to find a female, one whom had been 'De-Flowered' and to kiss her fully on the lips. But, I was warned, most severely, I had to drink the potion, the 'Juices of Testosterone' just before I kissed the lady. This was to protect her from catching the dread disease herself."
So, there it was! The way was clear now, for me to rid myself of the 'Raging Hormones' .
"Who do I kiss, my Lord?", I enquired, for I was not sure how I would know what lady had been 'De-Flowered" or, indeed, what 'De-Flowering' really was.
"You will remember a time when I informed you about the 'Red Rose'?"
I nodded, for I well remember the relief I felt when understanding that my sweet and sacred Alison was not to suffer the dreaded 'Raging Hormones', being aided by the magic of the 'Red Rose'.
"Well then 'Runt of a rodent', any lady who has been open to the 'Red Rose' is 'De-Flowered'!"
"Indeed, wisest of all beings, but how will I know if the lady has been 'De-Flowered'?"
'He who walks the heavens' raised himself once more, now seemingly impatient with my questioning.
"Because, 'Pimple-Winkle', she will obviously be older than you!...Now go. Be off with you!...And don't forget to deliver my message to Maureen, after giving my shoes a good polishing. Now go and close

the door. You can be quite tiring and I need to sleep." I rose, bowing low and, collecting his shoes, backed out of the door, closing it quietly, my mind awhirl with planning and calculations.

It has always struck me as rather strange, how shopkeepers subject all young boys to a watchful eye. Even stranger how the eagle-eyed nature becomes more suspicious when, with money in hand, a youth demands delivery.

"So you want one garlic bulb, one red chili and a small bottle of olive oil?"

For whose benefit these loud and outspoken words were for, I have no idea, though it would seem that these words caused the ladies, gathered into a queue behind me, to look at me with the same suspicious stare as I received from the shopkeeper. To my awareness now, there even seemed to be some murmurings from the women, which made me think that they understood my reason for being in the shop and my need of the items I held in my hand. Had I been more courageous, there is no doubt I would have explained that I was no 'Warlock', simply a boy who had no wish to be ravaged by the 'Raging Hormones'. Alas, having no courage, I lacked the voice and, with eyes downcast, left the shop in a hurried pace with my goods.

It is hard to be alone in the kitchen, for it seemed my father spent many fine hours there, wrapped up in his marital chores, his hands encased in the rubber of yellow gloves, an unhappy look about his face. However, as the day dragged into weariness, I at last heard my mother demand his presence, to announce they would be going out to see her mother, my Grandmother.

Time strolled its patient slowness, until I heard the street door shut, and so I aided time by quickly moving into the kitchen. This was a new territory to me. I knew where the tea-making equipment was, having been the tea-boy for 'He, who walks the heavens' since being of a height which allowed me to reach the top shelves. But now, opening and invading the drawers of the lower units was a baffling experience.
Ah, at last! Here was the cutlery-drawer, a division of knives, forks and spoons, And there, in a sectioned compartment, lay the very tool I sought, the small hammer I had once seen my small wizened father use when battering some meat into a flattened mess. Pocketing the prized object, I then took use of two small self-sealing bags and a small test-tube-like bottle which had a cork stopping its neck.
Like a thief in the night, I crept back up to my room with my swag and there I lay on my bed and waited.

"Why are you not at school?"
In some sort of shock, my mind startled itself awake, my eyes, in blurred awareness, saw the large figure of my mother at the foot of my bed. Slowly, my mind worked, sorting time into perspective and realizing that, lying on my bed, waiting for the evening to draw in, I had fallen asleep.
Doubtless, my torment of the early morning discovery of a second 'Zit', plus the 'Telling of Secrets' from 'He who walks the heavens', had a tiring effect. And so, here I lay, shocked in discovery that I had not been to school.
It is inherent in every young boy's make-up, that deception, escapism and excuses are a natural talent. There is no thought, no dam which holds back the seepage of intelligence. Generally, the mechanism triggers off a facial twitch, which then assumes a pose that gains a sympathetic understanding. Thus I turned sorrowful eyes upwards.
"I am ill, my mother.", I said.
With surprising speed, my mother came to my side and, laying a hand upon my brow, considered me to have no fever. It is strange how women use this maneuver, to feel another's brow in such an emergency. It is not in a man's intelligence, to test the heat of another's distress, so, in this sense, it is far easier to deceive the male mentality when effecting this excuse.
"Indeed… I feel a bit better, my mother. Perhaps the

sleep helped me rid myself of any further upset."
Was that disbelief in her eyes, that momentary hesitance which caused her to examine me with a further inspection before accepting my falsehood.?
I breathed a sigh of relief as my mother left, closing the door behind her.

I settled myself down to await for a time when I knew school would be out and I might see Spotty Watson. It is a known fact that a secret carried alone is a hard task, for one is forever fighting with one's nature, to share the intelligence. So it was considered to be far easier to me, that I share my secret with my very best and true friend, Spotty Watson, understanding that this 'Telling' would be kept in confidence. I lay on my bed, awaiting the lengthening of shadows.
Awake now to plans, I gave it the time before I crept down the stairs, stopping to listen to any sound which might warn me of any parental approach.

Before making my way to Spotty Watson's house, I would make my promised 'Duty' call, stopping at the house a few doors down and knocking on the door. The Lady Maureen Soap was, indeed, beauty intensified and I felt my breath catch hold in my throat when this divine creature opened the door.
"Well?... What is it?"
I averted my eyes, trying to summon up the breathe to voice my errand. It came, the stricture so reluctant

to release its hold that my voice wheezed and croaked its intent.

"My… Lord… is ill."

"Your Lord?...What on earth are you mumbling about, you silly child?"

Had this wondrous creature realized I was caught in the throes of the 'Raging Hormones', there was no doubt she would have softened her tone. But, ignorant of that fact and seemingly uncaring of my awkwardness, she put hands to hips and glared at me, before closing the door in my face.

I felt I had carried out my end of the bargain, my sainted elder sibling's wish that I inform the Lady Maureen Soap of his ill-health and so, in this conscience-free state, I set myself to the task of acquainting Spotty Watson with my plan of action for the next day, a day which I decided to call, 'The day of action!'

"You were not at school today.", said Spotty Watson, on opening the door to my knocking.

His eyes had a disapproving look in them as he made this statement. I could understand his accusation, because we had always shared our comings and goings, as is within the rules of the 'Sacred Blood'.

"Spotty", I announced. "I have some amazing and extraordinary revelations to make."… Here, I looked round darkly, assuring myself that there was no-one who might hear the conversation. Spotty followed my looks, his face now taking on a most interested and enthusiastic look. With that, he drew me into the house by the arm, putting his finger to his lips for silence and we climbed the stairs to his bedroom. There, now seated upon his bed I first made Spotty join me in the 'Blood pact', that what I tell him should never be divulged to any other, on pain of death. I would like to tell you what this ceremony composed of, but this cannot be done.

Having acted out the 'Pact', I then acquainted my very best friend with all the known facts of the case, of my sainted elder siblings search for the Guru and the secret of the 'Juices of Testosterone'.

I must admit here, dear readers, that it is every young boys right to embellish any tale and so, with hearty gestures and theatrical voice, I embellished the telling, even more so, when I saw the white roundness of Spotty Watson's eyes give stark contrast to the blue marbles of his pupils behind the glasses.

As I told the 'Telling', my fingers formed the 'Sacred Tent', finger-tips touching, with thumbs solidifying the shape. I noted, too, that, whether by subconscious copying, or a wish to join me with a same intention, Spotty Watson's hands joined, to erect the same shape, thus securing the secret deep within our souls.

There was a longest silence while Spotty Watson digested my 'Telling'. Until...

"So what is your plan?", he asked

“My plan is to find a woman who has been ‘De-Flowered’ and to drink the ‘Juices of Testosterone’ before kissing her”
“Gosh!”, exclaimed Spotty, his eyes wide in admiration. “ You mean to walk up to any woman, a complete stranger in the street and then kiss her?”
His words, in the cold light of day, poured limitless cold water on my enthusiasm. I had not considered this part of the plan. Was it to be that my ‘Day of Action’ was to be ruined through a lack of planning. We sat in silence for some time, each in our own thoughts.
“Why does it have to be a woman?”, asked Spotty.
“Because I cannot see a man being ‘De-Flowered’, Spotty”, I retorted.
“No…What I meant was, why does it have to be an old woman, why not a girl?”
“What girl? We have to know the girl is older than myself, to be sure she has been ‘De-Flowered’”.
Spotty Watson considered my statement, his eyes narrowing until, assessing an answer, his eyes widened.
“What about that new girl… Alison…In our class!”, he exploded, and continued, the excitement lighting his face. “We know already she is a month older than you. Ergo, she has been ‘De-Flowered’!”

My whole world, which had been darkened, now livened itself in an excited glow of colours. How I marveled at my very best friend’s intelligence, now knowing for certain that he had inherited the genetic mentality of his father, the 'Teller of Tall tales'. Would I kiss you, Spotty Watson, had I been more exuberant, but my reserved nature constrained this action. Nevertheless, should ever Spotty Watson be called upon to fight for honour, it will be me who will kneel in his stead, in a night of vowed silence before such a courageous act! If there be any fair maiden in this land that I would willingly kiss, then that maiden would be the sweet and most desirable Alison.

"We have to consider a course of action.", said Spotty, gazing at my face, before continuing. "While the maturity of walts and ulcerations are an attractive feature to a woman, it has to be considered that the sight of immature 'Zitlets' can have an opposite effect. The remedy is to camouflage your spots with make-up, so they do not turn Alison against you."
I was so in agreement with my very best friend that I nodded heartily to all he said.
"Tomorrow morning, at an early light, I shall wake you by throwing a stone at your bedroom window. You will let me in and I shall have with me the make-up, borrowed from my mother's dressing-table, with which I will apply, so you appear normal. Then I shall leave you, to wait till school-time, when you will come into the class and, there, kiss Alison."

Such an excellent plan!

Spotty Watson was, indeed, the son of the 'Master'. In fact, I would go as far as to say that Spotty Watson was not too far behind his father when it came to planning and scheming.
I left his house with an air of one who is a happiest of men, a stoutest of hearts.
And tonight, I would apply myself to the preparation of the 'Juices of Testosterone'!

Moonlight and owl-hooting, the soft rustle of leaves to a sighing wind, are not noises of a young boys education. Night-times are for the comfort of adventurous dreams and soft eiderdowns, of snoring and the occasional passing of wind. Thus, the night sounds, sights and smells, were new to my experience as I moved quickly, hugging shadows, on my way to the Meadow Park. The Meadow Park was not my ideal playground in the daytime, so that this, in the dead of night, with only a moon's rays for light, needed all my courage to move me onwards. The very fact that, seated in the center of the park, stood a large and spreading oak tree, the very tree which would afford me sanctuary while I prepared the potion, the 'Juices of Testosterone', was the spirit of my movement. On reaching the tree, I sat, my back against its wide trunk and began to make preparation. In concentrated effort, I poured some of the Olive Oil into the glass tube and corked it, before taking out the rest of the paraphernalia. Using the

hammer, I crushed the two garlic clothes and red chili into a mashed concoction, stuffing them with a stubby forefinger into the tube and, re-corking, then gave the tube a solid shaking.
The job done, I made sure to give my blessings to this sacred tree, closing one eye, I softly recited the words which I and Spotty Watson held sacred…

" Hand on heart, hand on head,
May I wind up very dead,
May I only have one eye
If I ever tell a lie."

As I said these words, I accentuated their meaning by carrying out the actions, by placing my hand, first on my heart, then on my head and, lastly, holding the hand over my left eye so that my right eye was the only one sighted. High above me, the owl hooted, the hoot turning into a screech as it dived down, zooming in on a reckless shrew which had diced with death for a meal. Jumping up in alarm and forgetting to take my hand away from my eye, I stared round wildly. The kill made, quietness and my sense of panic returned.
As I came, so I left, creeping off into the dead of night, to gain the security of my home and the comfort of a warm bed, the magic 'Juice' safely hidden beneath my pillow.

It seemed that I had only just closed my eyes when the sound of small stones hitting the window woke me. Normally, I like to lay there, soaking in the daylight through closed eyelids; then, as Spotty Watson and I had put into our 'Gang Rulebook', it was important to open and close the eyes six times, in quick succession. This procedure was to insure us against any ill-wills the day might hurl at us. Generally, this practice seemed to work quite well, except against the 'Raging Hormones', from which there seemed to be no know charm or 'Lucky Escape' mechanism.

However; this morning, the 'Eye-Day-Charm' was not even considered as I quickly crept down the stairs and let Spotty Watson in. Once back in my bedroom, he laid out the materials, taken from a bag he carried under his arm.

"Do I wash first, Spotty?", I asked.

"Of course not, especially if you are going to have make-up applied. My father says that a woman leaves the grime on, so that the grease in make-up does not slide off the face, dirt acts as a sort of base-coat. Anyway, father says that only dirty people wash."

I fully agreed. Here again, what Spotty Watson's father says, only shows again the remarkable sense that man has.

I sat as Spotty began by applying a base of white paste. Whatever it was, I felt its coldness, then the strange sensation of my skin seeming to stretch then tighten, so that it seemed my face-skin was unable to move. I tried to smile but I heard a creaking, which stopped me in my tracks.

“Is it all right, Spotty?”, I asked nervously.

“Be quiet, or it will crack.”, replied this ‘Master of Arts’, so I sat patiently while he meticulously worked on each part of my face, the tip of his tongue poking out. At times he stopped, tilting my face this way and that as he studied the results. There were times when he nodded an acceptance, and others, when he shook his head and began with another colour.

It is amazing, and I had never realized, how awkward it must be for a woman to have another apply facial make-up, without following the applier with her eyes. My eyes swiveled from side to side, following Spotty’s movements as he worked.

At last he stood back to admire his handiwork.

“One last dab.”, he decided, coming forward, to dab on some more colour.

“There.”, he said, satisfied at last.

I went to ask if I might look into a mirror and found, to my horror, that I could not move my lips, my face seemed set in concrete.

“Don’t move yet.”, instructed Spotty. “Let the paint dry.”

My eyes seemed to be the only free-moving part of my face and these I rolled in a most imploring way.

“And don’t speak, otherwise you break the spell, the magic.”

Ah!…That made sense. I should have known that Spotty would have spent a good part of the night chanting, to insure this worked on the day. 'Juju Magic' and 'Chanting' was a very important part of life, as every boy knows.

"Anyway.", insisted Spotty… "There is no need to speak. The idea is to kiss Alison and then, you may say whatever comes into your head."

How I admired this boy, my very best friend and fellow member of our 'Gang'. But his brain, as I stated earlier, was genetically inherited from the 'Teller of Tall Tales.'.

"Don't forget to sit and let it all dry. And wait here till it is time for school before coming out. Then it is all in your hands, dear friend."

I watched him leave, sly in his 'Sidling' as he crept down the stairs and out of the house.

I held back my silent tears. Should any boy have a friend as good and as stout-hearted as Spotty Watson, then he is, indeed, a lucky boy. I felt my heart well up in emotive swell and fought hard to hold back the tears which seemed to want to dampen my eyes and spill onto the fresh paint. I sat in resolute coldness, not allowing my feelings to get the better of me…I sat as the paint dried and sounds of the house-tenants awoke.

I listened in quiet solitude as I heard my mother talking to my father in a loud voice. She called him 'Norman'. I tried not to giggle, my insides hurting as I clutched at them… 'Norman'… I had never heard his name before. I began to think of names… ‘Un-Normal Norman’… ‘Nornamental’… ‘Norman the Hormone’…!

I was nearly on the floor in my merriment, clutching at myself, then sternly reminded myself that it was me who would be the laughing-stock of the whole wide world, should I break, both, the spell and the cast on my face.

I continued to sit on the chair, stone-faced and rather like the condemned man, alone and with his final thoughts. It was now, as I sat in the darkness of my mind that I realised how psychologically bad it is for any child who, even though misbehaving, is made to sit alone or to face the corner in solitude. The mind is a desperate thing, desperate for communication, derived from the need to be ‘Herdal’, the human being, an animal which thrives on close association and speech. These are the thoughts which ran through my head as I sat there, rather morbid and depressing. These are the kind of thoughts which a condemned man will have, and youths who suffer from the ‘Raging Hormones’. I thanked the ‘Lord’ for giving me an elder sibling, ‘He, who walks the heavens’. And for friends such as Spotty Watson and his father, the ‘Teller of Tall Tales’. I was born quite lucky, to have those around me who could guide me through this deadly time. Again, I felt the tears well up into my eyes and know that one or two teardrops rolled down my cheeks, even though I felt nothing through the thick mask of paint.

I listened as I heard my parents depart, the sound of a car start and the crunch of gravel on the driveway outside. It was nearly time for me to leave, to act in the biggest drama of my life. I rose from the chair and made my way to the mirror for a quick peek before leaving.

It was not me! It was not me!

I froze in horror! What stared back at me was a whitened face-mask, with large red clown-like splotches to my nose and both cheeks, while my eyebrows seemed raised in some eternal element of surprise. I was the 'Joker' from the 'Batman Comics'! I was 'Co-Co the Clown'!

My first instinct was to wash this hideous mask from my face, to live my life with the ravages of the 'Raging Hormones', till the disease dripped the last of my facial flesh from the bones, and onwards, till my brain became exposed as a riddled cheese-like object which scientists poured over. But even there, in my panic and through this 'Twilight Zone' of horror, love peered through, like the sun which pokes a sunny head over a grey cloud and lights the world up. Through my horrified state, I saw the smiling face of my adored and lovely Alison. She was my sun, I saw her beautiful eyes rise over the horizon of my fear, her cherry lips smile at me in a brilliance of light, and my horror abated as I knew that all this pain, this trial, was to be my entrance to heaven. I was being tested in my love for the beautiful Alison. Love, I knew, would see me through.

The time has arrived.

All was quiet beyond my bedroom door, pale in the dim light as I peeped out. I had reached the top of the stairs and, about to descend, when an apparition appeared behind me. I heard the slight swishing sound and turned quickly, to realize it was 'He, who walks the heavens'. He had come out from his room and was making his a yawning way towards the bathroom. His beautiful blue eyes, which had been half-closed, opened in a shocked horror, blazing like blue pearls as they took in my face. With no thought of his own safety, and instinctively using a form of self-protective 'Ju-Jitsu' move, he struck out, his push sending me tumbling backwards, down the full flight of the stairs.

It is said that we young boys are all arms and legs, and this is true, as I hurtled, like a 'Rag-Dolly' to my doom, arms and legs flapping wildly, while my mouth, released from its mask through an emergency of sound, screamed out in terror. I seemed to hurtle for an eternity, over and over, till, at last, with a resounding crash, I hit the hallway carpet at the bottom. For a time, I lay, as one does in a near-death situation, the brain sending nerve messages, to inspect all parts of the body in an emergency, so the messengers would return with an all-clear to the brain, or a message of pain, which informed the brain that things were not as they should be. My brain was informed that my body was wracked in shock, while an ankle-message reported a slight strain to the left-hand side. I was winded, in shock and with a pain to one ankle, but, apart from that, I seemed to be intact.

I thanked 'The Lord' for the suppleness of young bones.

"Are you mad!".

The thunder of grave fury descended and I lifted my eyes to see my sainted elder sibling coming at a fast gallop down the stairs, his eyes wide in a determined anger to punish me further.

Fear has a marvelous way of evaporating pain, and so it was with my pain, that, fearing the wrath of '’He, who walks the heavens', fear lent me wings as, rising to my feet, I accelerated to a speed way past the norm, evading capture and a certain torture, as I opened the street-door and ejected myself out into the street as does a cork which is ejected when 'Popped' from a Champagne bottle.

In determined style, I made my way to school, stopping only to assure myself that the tube, containing the magic 'Juice of Testosterone', was intact. I then continued, disregarding the looks I received from those I passed. The pain to my ankle seemed to deepen as I walked, so that I felt a certain relief if I walk in a sort of leg-dragging motion, one stout leg dragging the other behind it. In this fashion, I reached the gates of my school and made my way to my classroom, where, I was certain, the beautiful

Alison sat waiting for me. On reaching the door of my class, I could hear that the morning was well under way. Through the frosted glass I could make out Mr. Mates at his desk, his hand raised in a way which allowed him a sense of authority. I heard the buzz of voices and, with a deep breath, I pushed open the door and entered, dragging my lame foot behind me.

At first, as though in applause at my entrance, there was a deathly silence, a 'Silence' of admiration I might call it.

Then… There was pandemonium as screams of horror and shock came from the throats of those who stood in a frozen state. Mr. Mates had vanished, ducking under his desk. But my eyes were for the beautiful Alison. She sat still in her beauty, her eyes large and as round as pools of clear liquid. I moved in earnest, reaching her side and, kneeling, I removed the cork from the tube and drank deeply, taking in the 'Juices of Testosterone', before giving my beautiful Alison my 'Look of Love'.

Her mouth opened as I reached up to kiss her, my eyes wide in my 'Look', my pursed lips cracking the face-mask in a series of 'Popping' sounds as I moved ever closer. Suddenly, my eyes, which bulged with such passion as my 'Look of Love' allowed, bulged even more as they seemed to burst into flames, my breath steaming from my mouth in a fiery sense, as if I had taken on the being of a 'Dragon'. My whole stomach screamed in saturated heat, sending drastic illuminations of hellish lights from every orifice, the stench ascending to a higher heaven. The 'Juices of Testosterone' had set me on fire, causing me to scream in burning pain, while my backside erupted into a torment of devil's wind, even drowning out the screams which seemed to come from all around. I felt my innards lurch in a defiance, as they fought the instinct to retain the 'Juices' I had swallowed. My innards won the day and vomited the rejected mess, so that a stream of vileness exploded into Alison's lap.

And now there was another scream, a scream which seemed to come from a million miles away, while the open mouth of my beloved Alison seemed to open up like a cavern of hell.

Then I saw stars, literally, as Alison, in her fear, punched out at me, her fist closing my eye and causing such pain that my eye 'Blacked Out!'.

CHAPTER SIX.

‘THE ACCEPTANCE OF FATE.’

One might consider me fortunate in the outcome.
It had taken me three weeks to recover from the effects of my ill-health, from my sprained ankle and the after-effects of having the 'Juices of Testosterone' corrupt the workings of my innards.
My eye, too, was back to normal sight and normal colouring.
In other matters, I was reprimanded very severely by Mr. Tadworth, the Headmaster. Mr. Mates had been given a month's leave and, it appears, most of my class had received counseling and time off to recuperate. This last part being very much to my benefit, because I was now a much admired schoolboy for, what was considered to be, a greatest of pranks.
Of course, I held up my very best friend, Spotty Watson, as being the director of the piece and I only following the lead as cast by this most talented fellow.
The real tragedy was that my beautiful Alison was removed by her parents from the school, never to be seen again.
'He, who walks the heavens' never spoke of the incident, though there are times when his eyes reflected a kind smile on me, which lifted my heart to a highest heights.

"What you have been through, my boy, can have serious repercussions on you at a later stage in your life.", said Spotty Watson's father, easing himself back into the chair.
From the kitchen came the sound of the 'Happy Woman', Spotty Watson's mother, who busied herself among the pots and pans.
I sat, alongside Spotty Watson, in our usual position, on the floor before the seated 'Teller of Tall Tales'.
My day had begun when I first arose and, on entering the bathroom, I began to hum a few bars of a song which contained rather an amusing chorus about 'Three old Ladies locked in a lavatory'. The day earlier, my voice, high in youthful peculiarity, began to crack and somehow wobble, so that it could not attain the perfection sought.
Of course, I had gargled. In fact I had gargled many times, often, after drinking the foul 'Juices of Testosterone'. The taste had a most lingering disenchantment, clinging, not only to the roof of my mouth and spoiling any intake of food, but seeming to spill itself out with each breath. I might tell you, the doctor, on examination of me at the earlier time, disclosed to my mother that I was suffering from a case of halitosis.

But I digress…

The fact was, I found that each time I now spoke or

sang, my voice took on a see-saw effect, one minute high, the next, somewhat lower, as if unsure of itself. I, too, noticed a few more pimples had disgraced themselves, peppering my skin in such a way that Spotty Watson suggested if we joined the spots together, there might be some coded drawing waiting to be discovered. I had allowed my very best friend to do this, but to our dismay, only found that the joined spots resembled more of a spider's web than any picture.

It was, after discussion between myself and Spotty Watson, we decided to beg an audience before the 'Teller of Tall Tales'. This seeking was granted on a very fine Saturday morning, after the 'Nature Program' about Honey Bears, had finished…

And here we sat as Spotty Watson's father continued to speak…

"The mind and body are a most marvelous machine, working together so that adulthood is perfected. But sometimes the metamorphic process, which produces the butterfly from the childish caterpillar, becomes blocked and the messages from the brain to certain glands are not received, so the glands do not allow harmonic juices to flow."

I sat there, unsure about what this great man was saying, though sure that this was, indeed, a speech of pure genius.

"I will now tell you something, young fellows.", he went on. Spotty and I leaned ever forward, so that we miss nothing of what was being explained.

"Think of all your great achievers, your men of vision, artists, painters, architects, authors, your inventers, what have they all got in common?"

Both Spotty and I wracked our small brains, summoning up images of people such as Albert Einstein and Reubens.

I will say, I found the paintings of Ruebens quite fascinating. Having recently taken an interest in art and visiting the public library a number of times on secret missions, I found this artist had a fine eye for detail. His drawings and paintings of women were perfection and quite inspired my thinking and secret dreams. How lucky he must have been, to have such voluptuous ladies model for him. I had decided to become an artist, once I had overcome the 'Raging Hormones'.

I also found that 'The Raging Hormones' had another strange effect, in that it caused my mind to wander from the point, so that I often seemed to be in a daze. Like now, for some considerable time, while my eyes were glued to Spotty Watson's father's face, seeing his mouth open and close as he spoke, I did not hear his voice, instead, only seeing the images of naked Reubenesque ladies, floating above the realms of mental vitality. In a determined pull of concentration, I lost sight of the naked visions, in time to hear Spotty Watson's father say…

"… And so imagination is the visionary skin which stays the flow of minerals, salts and juices, which are ejected at certain times from the glands, rather like the skin which grows over any foreign body, thereby causing spots or worse. This stoppage, this action, then has the re-action of causing the 'Raging Hormones'. It stops the effectiveness, the ease that is natural to evolved growth."

If I gained the correct sense of what his great man was saying, those with a grand sense of imagination have bodies which are less likely to accept the changes which go on in times such as the 'Raging Hormones'. I was not about to ask if I were correct in my assumption, but I knew then, I would have to reign in the visions of imagination I was receiving. I also recalled, at an earlier meeting with Spotty Watson's father, that those earlier men of vision were never really happy in their lives. This thought was somewhat depressing, in that I, with a grand sense of imagination, would be an unhappy soul. Perhaps this is why my father, ever unhappy, spent much of his time, imagining he was elsewhere, rather than in the confines of the kitchen, his hands immersed in bowlfuls of hot, soapy, water.

"Is there, Sir, a way in which I might rid myself of an overload of imagination?", I said.

"The problem is, my boy, you are already in the throes of the 'Raging Hormones', it has you in its grip. It is always better to catch a lad at an early age, before the mind is allowed any fanciful visions."

I digested the answer.

"So nothing can be done. I am too late?"

As I said these words, my voice broke to a lower

tone, as if accepting the feeling of hopelessness which lowered itself into the pit of my stomach.
"I am afraid you will have to undergo 'The Acceptance of Fate'", said Spotty Watson's father, at the same time picking up a newspaper and, with a belch, began to read. This Spotty Watson took as a sign of dismissal and, rising to our feet, bade us leave 'The Teller of Tall Tales' to his reading..

In a miserable silence, Spotty Watson and I wandered our way down the street, until Spotty exclaimed…

"I have an idea!"

I am always quick in hope and this exclamation, ejected from my very best friend's lips, surged the spirit of enthused hope through my bones.
"What is it Spotty?"
"There is a shop in the High Street which sells scented candles and herbs, as well as old books and things. Perhaps we can find something there which can help you solve the problem of the 'Raging Hormones."
Whether the shop had any answers did not matter, I needed an injection of hope and so we made our way to this establishment.
Spotty Watson's father had once said that atmosphere was everything, especially to those with a vivid imagination. This I found to be quite true, for, as we

entered the shop, I felt the hairs rise at the nape of my neck, the sights and scents already conjuring up visions of an old witches cave. It also made me think of 'He who walks the heavens' for some reason, then determined the scent from the candles, of pine and sandalwood, were the same smells which came from the candles in his room. This was indeed eerie, in that I might have stumbled across the same shop as my sainted elder sibling used.

"Can I help you young lads?"

The voice startled me from my thoughts.

"We want to look at your books, the ones with spells in them.", said Spotty, in an almost defiant way.

The shop-keeper, an elderly man with a stoop, smiled, secure in his age.

"We don't actually sell books of that nature. We are not the Occult. But…", he went on. "We do have some books on Medieval Knights and tales of that nature"

"Do you have any books on art?", I asked, hopefully.

"No, I'm sorry. You can find those kind of books in a proper bookshop or in the library."

I turned away, my attention taken up by a model which stared down at me from one of the shelves. It was a statue of Medusa, an ugly old crone who had snakes growing out from her head. My mind began to wander, back to what 'He who walks the heavens' had once said about women, and how, with one look, they might rob you of 'The Snake that wriggles', using it as a lock of their hair and, thus, robbing you of your strength. I counted the snakes and found that this statue had nineteen 'Snake-locks'. I found this to be quite a mystery, for I really had no idea what a 'Snake that wriggles was', or how any woman could fasten it to their head.

"Look!"

Spotty, as becomes a swat, had been reading through the pile of old books and now held one up, his face wreathed in a smile of triumph.

"What is it, Spotty?"

"Read the title."

"The Act of Acceptance.", I read.

The book cover held a picture of a knight, kneeling before an alter, his hands together as in prayer.

"Don't you see!", exclaimed Spotty.

"As my father said, you have to learn the 'Acceptance of Fate! And here we have this book, right at hand, which explains how one can master the 'Art of Acceptance'."

Spotty's enthusiasm sparked its way through me, sending a shiver of pulses up into my brain.

Of course, fate has led us to this shop.!

Thinking on it, each step of the way had been leading me to a final glory!

The old shop-keeper, who had been listening to our vibrant speech of exaltation and had been staring over Spotty's shoulder at the book, took it away from Spotty and weighed it in his hand.

"How much is that book?", demanded Spotty

"As you can see, it is quite a rare and valuable book,

in good condition, considering its age."

It is strange, with old shop-keepers, how they all take on this Shylock appearance when determining money is to be made. And so it was with this one, who seemed to stoop even lower, his face taking on a most sinister grimace.

"Well? How much?"

Spotty was undeterred and spoke with such authority that I felt it my duty to stand alongside this valiant youth in his bargaining.

"How much?", I echoed, pulling out what little change I had in my pocket.

"I will do you a deal.", said the old man.

"A deal?... What sort of deal?", asked Spotty.

"I f you two lads stack up all the books and tidy the back room for me, I will let you have this most valuable book for nothing. Do we have a deal?"

The back room of the shop was an experience of hard labour. There is no doubt, no-one had seen the dust-laden items for many weeks, but we set ourselves to the task and the dust flew.

As good as his word, the old shop-keeper was almost genial in his blessings and handed over the book to Spotty, who clasped it under his arm, never releasing his grip till we had reached his bedroom.

"You read it, Spotty.", I said, allowing he was the better reader. I spread myself out on his bed as he seated himself in the broken rocking chair, which creaked to the momentum as he began to read.

I personally cannot advise you of the reading, word for word, for that would stretch your patience and my writing hand to its limit. However, I would advise you all, should you ever get the chance to purchase the said book, 'The Act of Acceptance', then you should do so, for it contains many excellent facets of escape mechanisms, which might come in useful to anyone facing fears, imagined or otherwise.

And so, Spotty read on…

And here, I will give you the 'Gist' of what this book is about.

It would seem that a certain Arthurian knight, Sir Valiant De L'Eau Noir, had involved himself in an affair with two ladies of the court. It would appear that Knights of that time were forbidden to enjoy such a liaison and, being discovered, he was ordered to go into the forest, and there to seek out a 'Raging Dragon', a fierce monster with the purpose of killing it, so saving a local populace from certain destruction. The story went on to state that, because of the Knight's behavior, he was doomed to failure. Failure meant the knight would, on his honour, fall on his own sword, to die, unless, of course, he found a way to kill the 'Raging Dragon'.

The story continued, stating that the knight spent a whole night in vigil, kneeling at an alter in prayer, refusing to eat or sleep. And while at his vigil, an Angel appeared, to tell him what he must do if he was to win his battle with such a fearsome beast. He would have to perform an 'Act of Acceptance'. This meant he would have to don a 'Knight's Hood', explained as a kind of skull-cap which was veiled, and, wearing this, he was to seek out each of the fair maidens he had loved, then to kiss each on the cheek, vowing never to see either again, not even in death.

With this action of 'Acceptance', the Knight would go on to defeat the 'Raging Dragon' and become a hero, saving himself and the townsfolk from certain destruction. The story concluded the knight rode off, into the sunset, ever to ride in search of adventure, but never to win another lady's heart.

Spotty snapped the book shut, laying on the bed beside me and we lay in silence, examining our own thoughts as to what the book meant to us.

"You know what this means?", said Spotty suddenly, breaking into my thoughts.

"What does it mean, Spotty?"

"Don't you understand the 'Secret!"

Spotty jumped up from the bed, his face alive with excitement.

"What is it, Spotty? What have you found?", I cried, jumping up to join him in an excited state.

"Well, don't you see? The 'Raging Dragon' is just another way of saying the 'Raging Hormones!"

"Oh, my Giddy Aunt, Spotty, of course it does!"
The thing was, even though I jumped about in such a state of excitement, I still had not the slightest idea what Spotty was going on about. Pride, in its most obstinate fashion forbid me to pursue the truth of what Spotty was saying, so I simply kept exclaiming…"Oh, my Giddy Aunt!"…, over and over again, until Spotty continued.
"It's so simple, you see. Though you have to kiss a lady who has been 'De-Flowered', it does not have to be a young girl. In the book it shows that the Knight has to kiss two ladies who had been sullied, each one on the cheek. That's the answer!"
"Explain further, Spotty.", I begged.
"Well, what you have to do is spend a night in vigil. That means kneeling by your bed all night, with your hands in prayer, as it shows in this picture.".
Here, Spotty held up the book, showing me the cover picture of the Knight in vigil.
"You have to prayer for deliverance and 'Acceptance', so you will be delivered from the ravages of the 'Raging Hormones'."
"Then what do I have to do, Spotty, I mean, after I have spent the night in prayer and vigil?"
"What you have to do is, first, find yourself a 'Knight's Hood', a sort of hat with a veil. Then go out and find two ladies to kiss, one on each cheek, swearing never to darken their paths again, even in death. Then simply wait for the 'Acceptance', the end of the 'Ravaging Hormones,!"

My mind whirled, it cried out in thankfulness to this dear and stalwart friend, who had seen through the coded words of the book and, thus, delivered me from the ravages of the 'Raging Hormones'.
"Spotty, my friend…I salute you!", I cried, bestowing on him the highest praise one 'Gang-Member' can give to another.
"And I receive it in honour!", returned Spotty, throwing a clenched fist across his chest as is written in our 'Gang-Book', in reception of such an honour.

In the way of high excitement, my head brimming with an opulence of ideas, I made my way home. All was quiet as I entered, and I wished it to remain that way as I raided the refrigerator and wolfed down whatever took my fancy. I needed to fill my innards, for tonight I would be in deep deprivation, starving myself of the life-giving food which every young boy needs.
It was as I was half-way up the stairs when the idea struck me, the brilliance of this sudden lightning-bolt causing me to gasp. I stood, allowing the breath to be drawn into my body, before continuing my climb. The door creaked as I opened the door to my parents bedroom and I first ran my eyes around the room before entering. Closing the door, I switched on the light and went to the wardrobe. There, seated on its highest shelf, sat the box I wanted. Bringing it to the bed, I opened the box and withdrew the 'Wedding Hat'.

My mother adored this hat, a large red affair, wide-brimmed with copious amounts of feathers acting as a foliage, a hedge of colour. Mother called it her 'Wedding hat' because she only wore it at weddings, and, to my mind, in view of her great age, she would not be using it too much. Anyway, should she know of my need, surely, in her love for me, she would not begrudge me the use of it.

Replacing the empty box on top of the wardrobe, I took a pair of scissors from the dressing table, along with some safety-pins, then stealthily made it back to my own bedroom.

With great care I removed the feathers from the hat, pushing them to a hidden retreat beneath my bed.

Next, with a same dexterity, I trimmed the brim away from the hat so that it took on the appearance of a red flower-pot. Going to my cupboard, I sought out and found the fishing nets and cut the nets from their holdings. In fastidious fashion, I used the safety-pins to fasten the nets around the brim of the hat.

There! The 'Knight's Hood' was made!

I tested it on my head, allowing the net to cover my face, looking into the mirror and was very pleased with the reflection which gazed back at me.

Wearing my 'Knight's Hood' and with a confidence way beyond that of a lad my age, I knelt beside my bed, elbows resting, my hands flat to each other in prayer. I closed my eyes and began praying…The vigil had begun.

It is rather strange, that, in this kneeling position, with my head full of prayers and angelic visions, I became quite light-headed. Somewhere, high up in the altitude of reason, I was aware of slight noises and house-sounds. I had no idea of time or sensibility, yet I heard a car in the drive, a door closing, drifting voices which disappeared into a kaleidoscope of colours…
Then I saw the Angel. She drew into my vision from a side entrance, a butterfly shape at first, then customising herself into a form of pure beauty.
I watched her dance, to sing and laugh, moving round me and, as she moved, there as left a stream of velvet stars which burst into scarlet bubbles. I was bathed in silent wonder. Then she stopped her movements and walked towards me, her face in beauty. She came nearer, laughing now, laughing as her eyes got bigger.
Then a blinding flash as the whole vision exploded. I shouted out, feeling the bite of tragic disappointment. I kept my eyes closed, searching the darkness. There was nothing, except the sound of laughter, a distant noise of hilarity which has lost its beautiful music. I opened my eyes.

I had no idea of the time, it was dark, I knew that it was well into the evening. My body felt stiff and I lifted myself onto the bed, removing the 'Knight's Hood' and laying it down. Was it all a dream? I doubted that, the angel was a truth, as it was in the book. Again I heard laughter ring out, distant but plain and I realized it came from downstairs. Opening the door, I listened, then, creeping to the head of the stairs, I peered down. I made out the sound of my mother talking. She laughed and was joined by another voice, who also joined in the laughter. I knew the other voice belonged to Martha Evergreen-Stokes, my mother's best friend.

My mind froze to the realization that here was the very chance, fate had lead me to this ending, this act of finality which would give me the chance to put myself to the 'Act of Acceptance' and finalise the deed of honour.

Returning to my bedroom, I replaced the 'Knight's Hood' back on my head, making sure the net was down to veil my face. With soft, but fearless steps, I made my way down the stairs and then walked into the lounge.

The talking and laughter ceased. My mother sat, tea-cup and saucer in her hands and, like Martha Evergreen-Stokes, she sat stoned in silence, her eyes wide, as was her mouth. In good grace, I moved to my mother's side and, bending, I moved the veil of the 'Knight's Hood' to one side so that my lips lightly touched my mother's cheek. Straightening, I turned and committed the same act to the cheek of the silent Martha Evergreen-Stokes.

There was not a sound, pure blissful silence as I walked back to the doorway and turned, to look at

them both from behind the veil.
“My dear ladies.”, I said, my voice so calm and so deep. “My kiss to you both is a last token of my respect to you. From this day forth, I shall never darken your path again. Not even in death.”

Regaining my bedroom, I removed the ‘Knight’s Hood’, setting it gently on the floor beside the bed. I then lay myself onto the bed, stretched out with my arms folded across my chest. I closed my eyes and waited for the time to come…
I had committed the ‘Act of Acceptance’ and now knew the ‘Raging Hormones’ would be laid to rest.

FINIS.

www.ingramcontent.com/pod-product-compliance
Ingram Content Group UK Ltd.
Pitfield, Milton Keynes, MK11 3LW, UK
UKHW020149200726
13856UKWH00003B/909